1A The Wool Market Dyer  
An imprint of Memo

Thwarted: 978-1-86151-523-0

First published in Great Britain in 2015
by Mereo Books, an imprint of Memoirs Publishing

The address for Memoirs Publishing Group Limited can be found at
www.memoirspublishing.com

The Memoirs Publishing Group Ltd Reg. No. 7834348

The Memoirs Publishing Group supports both The Forest Stewardship Council®
(FSC®) and the PEFC® leading international forest-certification organisations. Our
books carrying both the FSC label and the PEFC® and are printed on FSC®-certified
paper. FSC® is the only forest-certification scheme supported by the leading
environmental organisations including Greenpeace. Our paper procurement policy
can be found at www.memoirspublishing.com/environment

Typeset in 10/15pt Century Schoolbook
by Wiltshire Associates Publisher Services Ltd. Printed and bound in Great Britain
by Marston Book Services Ltd, Oxfordshire

The best laid schemes o' mice and men
Gang aft a-gley,
An' lea'e us nought but grief an' pain
For promis'd joy.

Robert Burns (1759-96) Scottish poet and songwriter

# CHAPTER ONE

Regimental Sergeant Major Robert Carson MC, of the 1$^{st}$ Battalion, the Essex and Hertfordshire Light Infantry Regiment, and his wife, Valerie, were being dined out of the battalion Warrant Officers' and Sergeants' Mess on the occasion of his retirement. The guests included the battalion commander, Lieutenant Colonel Bernard Deacon, the battalion adjutant, Captain Justin Barker, and the four company commander majors.

The dinner was over and the mess members and their guests were listening to their commanding officer's laudatory speech about Carson's distinguished service career during times of peace and war.

As the Colonel sat down on Carson's right, the mess members broke into song: *'For he's a jolly good fellow, and so say all of us. For he's a jolly good fellow, and so says all of us, and so say all of us.'* This was followed by groups of the now convivial mess members and guests recalling their service experiences with Carson.

The Colonel turned to Carson. 'Well, now that your last day in the Army has arrived, what are your plans for the future, for you and Valerie, Bob?'

Our plans have been well laid, sir. We're emigrating to Australia to join our daughter, Janice, and our grandchildren. It's been more than five years since we've seen her and we've never seen our grandchildren, the twins, Bruce and Wendy.'

'Yes, with all those deployments to trouble spots, it must have been difficult for you to arrange a visit to your family.'

'It was also the expense involved in getting there. It wasn't because I was hard up, but my son-in-law Ben, who is Australian, is a master builder. He was building a bungalow for the family and I was sending him all our spare cash to help pay for the work.'

'Do you plan to live with them?'

'Oh, yes, sir. Ben's already drawn up plans to build an extension to the bungalow to provide accommodation for us.'

'My word, you do have a useful son-in-law.'

'Yes, he certainly is. I'm going to see that he's paid for all the materials and work involved.'

'I know a warrant officer's pension for thirty-seven years' service is quite a tidy sum, but the gratuity you get, which will amount to three years' pension, won't go far if you're planning to pay for the extra building work. Not only that, the cost of living in Australia is higher than it is here.'

'I know, that's what Ben has told me. My annual pension will be about twenty-one thousand, so I should get a sixty-three grand terminal gratuity.'

'Do you intend to try to get a job out there?'

'No, there's little chance of finding work at my age. They

only want skilled tradesmen and professionals, such as teachers and engineers. All I can offer them is 39 years of soldiering. But Valerie is a qualified primary school teacher and she's only 51, so she might get a job. In fact Janice is making enquiries on her behalf. I also plan to look into investing my gratuity, which could increase our income.'

'Well, you do seem to have given your plans considerable thought. I hope everything turns out well for you and your family.'

'Thank you, sir. I hope so too.'

Turning to Valerie, who was sitting between Bob and Captain Barker, the Colonel said, 'I'm sorry, Mrs Carson, your husband and I have been rather neglecting you. I hope Captain Barker has been entertaining you with some of his more light-hearted army stories.'

Valerie turned to the Colonel with a smile. 'Oh, yes, Colonel Deacon, your adjutant is quite a comedian!'

The Colonel laughed. 'Yes, he certainly is. In fact he's one of the few people I know who can get soldiers laughing while they're under fire.'

It was past midnight before the party broke up, and there followed a period of handshaking and back-slapping goodbyes from the mess members and their guests.

A message came from the main guardroom that a taxi was waiting for Carson and his wife at the main gate to take them back to their married quarter, which was nearly a mile outside the barracks. Exhilarated by their warm send-off and their thought of their future with their family in Australia, they hardly felt the chill of the cold January night as they walked to the main gate.

# CHAPTER TWO

'Well, Mr Carson, you're now a fully-fledged member,' said Mike Prentice, the secretary of the Romford branch of the British Legion, as he accepted Carson's completed application form and handed him a British Legion badge. 'Remember, if there is any help the Legion can do in assisting you to settle back into civilian life don't hesitate to see our welfare member.'

'Thanks, Mike, I'll remember that, but I don't think there's any help I need at the moment. That is, unless he has any knowledge about investing in the stock market.'

'Actually, our welfare member was a captain in the Army Pay Corps, so he might be able to give you some advice on financial matters.'

'I'll keep that in mind, Mike. Now, if you'll introduce me to your barman I'd like you to join me for a drink.'

'I can see we've got a new member with the right sort of spirit,' Prentice said with a wide grin. 'I'd be delighted. It'll give me the opportunity to introduce you to some of our members. You might even find an old comrade among them.'

Prentice led the way from his office to the bar and introduced Carson to the barman, a ruddy-faced, burly ex-corporal military policeman named Charlie Proust.

'What's yours, Mike?' asked Carson.

'A pint of best bitter will do me nicely, Bob. You don't mind me calling you Bob, do you? I know you were a regimental sergeant major and I was just a corporal when I left the army.'

'Of course not, Mike. We're no longer in the army, so call me what you like.'

'A pint of bitter for Mike, a large glass of your house red wine for me and whatever you'd like for yourself, Charlie,' Carson said, placing a twenty-pound note on the bar.

They sat chatting about their army service, and as members joined them at the bar Prentice introduced them to Carson, who did not know any of them.

Three drinks later, Prentice excused himself to attend to some paperwork in his office. Carson moved from the bar to sit on an easy chair, from which he could see the members entering and leaving the bar room.

He had finished his drink and was about to leave when a member approached him. 'Well, fancy meeting up with you here, RSM Carson. It must be twelve years,' he said as he sat in the chair next to Carson.

Carson immediately recognized him as a former sergeant, Roger Hurst, who had served with him in Iraq. Hurst had been court-martialled for ill-treating a prisoner-of-war and striking a superior officer    his company commander. He had been reduced to the ranks, awarded

112 days' detention and discharged with ignominy. Carson had been a prosecution witness at the court martial.

'Yes, Mr. Hurst. It is a surprise to see you as a member of the British Legion. I would have thought you would have broken off all connections with the army.'

Hurst retorted angrily. 'Oh, I see why you said that, you're harking back to my court martial. I still think I was well justified in giving that murdering Iraqi bastard a hard time when I was questioning him. He did kill two members of my platoon and refused to reveal the whereabouts of his unit.'

'I'm afraid I can't accept that as an excuse for your ill-treatment of a POW. Such prisoners are protected by the Geneva Convention. And striking a superior officer can't be justified either. You did break his nose!'

Hurst' eyes narrowed. 'Well, he and those bloody redcap SIB bastards were giving me a hard time and I had put a few drinks away before they pulled me in.'

Carson, wishing to end their conversation and leave the club, or at least change the subject, said, 'Well, let's put all that behind us and tell me what you're doing these days'.

Hurst' face softened. 'Oh, this and that, but I work mostly for finance companies as a debt collector. The pay isn't very much but I get commission on whatever I collect.'

'Hmm, that's not a very pleasant job, but I suppose someone's got to do it.'

'Yes, it's all right for people like you to talk like that, on an RSM's pension, but I was discharged without a pension, and with all the best jobs going to immigrants I have to take what job I'm offered.'

'Well, I suppose that's only to be expected. Generally

speaking the immigrants who come to this country looking for a new life are well-motivated, appropriately skilled and prepared to work hard for their living. Whereas you, Roger, are a former disgraced soldier whose only skill is soldiering.'

'I thought you'd say something like that,' Hurst replied.

'Oh, I'm sorry, Roger. Don't take it to heart. I wasn't trying to put you down. Let me buy you a drink as an apology. What'll you have?'

'If you're paying, Sergeant Major, a double Scotch would go down well.'

Carson gave a slight shrug. Then he walked to the bar and returned with the drink, which he placed on the sofa table in front of Hurst. 'Enjoy your drink, Roger. I'm off home now, goodnight.'

Hurst didn't reply, but he picked up the glass and took a long swig before muttering a near inaudible "thanks." As Carson left the room, Hurst gave his back a mock salute.

# CHAPTER THREE

Bob and Valerie Carson were having breakfast in their army married quarter. Their main topic of conversation was finding a house to rent until they were ready to emigrate to Australia.

'This looks like it will do for us,' Bob said, as he scanned the local newspaper. 'It's a two-bedroom furnished end terrace house in the centre of Romford.'

'What's the monthly rental?' Valerie asked, as she spread marmalade on her toast. 'I bet it'll be more than we want to spend on temporary accommodation.'

'No, I think the rent is quite reasonable. Anyway, we'll not be in it for long. My gratuity is now in our bank account, so as soon as I can find an investment that will provide a speedy profitable return, I'll send Ben the money he needs to make a start on the extension.'

'Then as soon as we've had another cup of tea, Bob, I suggest we pay a visit to the estate agent and arrange a viewing of the house.'

'Agreed, my dear, you make with the teapot and I'll give them a call.'

Bob rang the estate agent and asked if they could be shown over the advertised house. The agent agreed to pick them up from their married quarter and show them over the property that morning. The agent duly arrived, and within ten minutes they were on the way to Romford. They arrived in less than twenty minutes, and the agent led them to the last house in a terrace of late Victorian houses. They entered and the agent showed them around. The house appeared to be reasonably well maintained. The furnishings had all seen better days, but were adequate for their needs.

Both were pleased with what they saw and Bob agreed to take the house for twelve months. He exchanged a month's rent in advance and the customary deposit for the keys and told the agent that he intended moving in over the coming weekend. Carson's intention was to notify the garrison quartermaster and arrange to hand over their married quarter on the following Monday.

\*\*\*

That evening Bob and Valerie planned their move. They'd pack everything in the morning and Bob would arrange to hire a van and take their belongings to Romford. Then he and Valerie would spend a day putting everything away. Returning to the garrison, they would prepare their married quarter for inspection and hand over to the quartermaster on Monday morning.

Things went as planned and on Monday evening they opened a bottle of champagne to celebrate their first home together outside the army.

\*\*\*

After breakfast the following morning Bob trawled through the Yellow Pages, broadsheet newspapers and other publications that advertised financial advisers, consultants or investment brokers.

'Do you know what you're looking for, Bob?' asked his wife.

Bob sighed and ran his fingers through his thatch of iron-grey hair. 'Of course I do, but it's a matter of choosing the right one from the many.'

'Isn't there anyone you know who might be able to suggest a reputable firm?'

'No. Bankers, financiers and others who control the nation's money are not in favour in these times of financial crisis, so nobody wants to trust investment firms with their money.'

'Then you'll just have to use your judgement to select what seems to be a reliable firm that promises to provide a reasonable return on our investment. Now, if you'll excuse me, I'll get on with washing up the breakfast things,' Valerie said, as she went into the kitchen.

'Ah, this looks promising,' Bob called out. 'An investment firm called, Arkwright, Hislop and Pinder represent the Linduana Copper Mining Company, which is located in the Katanga Province of the Democratic Republic of Congo. They promise a high return on investments. Apparently the company has discovered a massive vein of copper and needs extra capital to develop the new source and extract the copper. It goes on to say that this find of copper will prove to be easier to extract and more profitable than the South

African goldfields.'

Valerie came into the sitting room, drying her hands on a tea towel. 'All that sounds almost too good to be true, but it's worth getting on to them.'

'I'll do it straight away and see if I can get more information about investing with them.'

Bob rang the firm and spoke to a young woman who announced herself as Sharon, Personal Assistant to the General Manager. She promised that one of their financial consultants would call on him that afternoon.

Bob and Valerie filled their morning by shopping for groceries, then had a hasty lunch in a high-street restaurant.

'We'd better be getting back,' Bob said, checking his watch. 'The secretary didn't give me a specific time for the arrival of their consultant, but my guess is he'll be here just after 1400 hours.'

'Fourteen hundred hours! Bob, now you're now back on Civvy Street, you really must drop all that military-speak. You should have said two o'clock, or just two.' She laughed.

'I know, my dear, but from the age of sixteen, when I entered Army Boys' Service, that's how I was taught to tell the time.'

At two-fifteen they were back at home and putting their groceries away when there was a ring at the front door. Bob opened it to see a suave-looking man in his mid-thirties, who reminded him of Errol Flynn, the hard-drinking, womanizing film actor. Carson had seen many of his films on television in his early youth.

The man produced a business card and handed it to Carson, who quickly read the details. 'Please come in, Mr

Rackman,' Carson said and led him into the sitting room, where Valerie was standing. 'Valerie, this is Mr Rackman. He's a financial adviser, and he's going to give us some information about investments.'

'I'm delighted to make your acquaintance, Mrs Carson,' Rackman said with a smile. He was quite a good-looking man, but a bit smarmy, thought Valerie.

'Well, if it's all right with you, Mr Carson, perhaps we can all sit down together and I'll put you in the picture regarding our current investments that are proving to be highly profitable in the short term,' said Rackman. He sat on an armchair and placed his briefcase on the sofa table. Bob and Valerie sat facing him on the sofa.

'Perhaps you could let me know how much you wish to invest and I can then let you have details of our best investments,' Rackman said, with a winning, toothy smile.

Bob massaged his chin in thought before replying. 'Well, er... I was thinking of investing most of the gratuity I received on my retirement from the army.'

'Oh, so you're an old soldier, then,' Rackman said with a wide grin. 'My company always likes to show its appreciation for the security the armed forces provide for our country. Our policy is to try to steer ex-servicemen to the best investments to suit their needs. So, what is the amount of your gratuity, Mr Carson?'

'It's sixty-three thousand pounds.'

'Hmm... that's a useful sum to invest.'

'I wouldn't invest it all. I want to keep a few thousand in the bank for any emergency that might arise.'

'I understand perfectly, Mr Carson. So, shall we say sixty thousand pounds is available for investment?'

Bob looked at Valerie. 'What do you think, dear?'

'Perhaps Mr Rackman could give us some idea of his company's best investments to think about before we decide how much to invest.'

'That's a very sensible attitude to take, Mrs Carson. I have details of our most promising investment with me.' He opened his briefcase and removed a file of papers. 'Your best option at this time is to invest with the Linduana Copper Mining Company, in the Democratic Republic of Congo. They've recently discovered an enormous...'

'Yes, I've read all about that in your advertisement,' Carson interrupted. 'What I should like to know is what sort of return we could expect to receive from our investment?'

Rackman spread his arms out. 'The sky's the limit. From the interest shown by our shrewdest investors we expect share prices to at least double in a few months. This is a golden opportunity for someone like you to become wealthy by doing nothing more than signing a few documents and placing your investment in our safe hands.'

'Well, Mr Rackman, I have to say you make it sound hard for anyone to pass up your offer,' replied Bob. 'However, I must stress that the success of any investment I make is most important. We need the extra money that it may earn to enable us to join our family in Australia.'

'Then you've nothing to worry about, Mr Carson. You can just sit back and see the share prices rise, and when your shares are worth the amount you need to emigrate, you can put them up for sale.'

'You make it all sound like money for jam, Mr Rackman,' said Valerie. 'But I believe my husband will agree that we need a little time to think over your proposal before we commit our capital. After all, many strange things happen in Africa.'

Rackman gave a low laugh. 'That may be so, but copper is an important mineral that is greatly desired by the fast-developing countries of the world, such as China, India and Brazil. This will improve the lives of the African peoples, so they are most unlikely to do anything to disrupt their copper mining industry. However, I quite understand your need to have a little time to think the matter over before you make your investment. Shall I return tomorrow with all the necessary paperwork, so that we can finalize your investment?'

'Oh, very well, Mr Rackman, we'll give the matter careful consideration and let you have our decision tomorrow afternoon.'

'Splendid! I'll return tomorrow at 3 pm. Goodbye, Mrs Carson.'

'Goodbye, Mr Rackman,' Valerie replied.

Rackman picked up his briefcase and followed Bob to the front door.

After Rackman had gone, Bob and Valerie looked through the brochure he had left for them to study.

'If this investment is as good as this brochure suggests, then we might as well go with it,' Bob said.

'Yes, but I have say there's something about Mr Rackman that I find rather dodgy.'

'Yes, I agree with you, he does come across like a used car salesman, but then most salesmen have that manner when they are trying to clinch a deal.'

'Yes, I'm sure you're right. I have to confess that while you were upstairs putting your clothes away, I logged onto the company's website and they seem genuine enough, but to be on the safe side, I suggest we limit the investment to fifty thousand.'

'Yes, I agree. You're usually right when it comes to money matters.'

***

Rackman arrived promptly the following afternoon and the share certificates were exchanged for a cashier's cheque for fifty thousand pounds.

'Now that's been done, Mr and Mrs Carson, you can sit back and watch the share price take off,' Rackman said, as he placed the cheque in his briefcase and rose to leave.

Bob and Valerie accompanied him to the door, where brief goodbyes were exchanged.

# CHAPTER FOUR

During the weeks that followed, Carson subscribed to the *Financial Times* and checked the daily movement of their shares. Their value moved upwards by a few pence for the first few weeks, then steadied for about a month.

Bob and Valerie read the news reports about Africa with increasing concern. It seemed anti-government insurgents had been rioting and demonstrating in the Democratic Republic of Congo. The situation had been further worsened by the infiltration of other anti-government rebel forces entering the country from the Central African Republic.

By early August the share price had started to fall. The Chief Executive Officer of the Linduana Copper Mining Company admitted that their early forecast of the amount of copper that could be extracted was overly optimistic. In spite of their enormous expenditure on the latest copper extracting equipment and the recruitment of many more miners, the yield of copper was negligible, and soon it petered out altogether. The share prices continued to fall, and during the month of September they crashed when the chief executive officer and two of his senior colleagues cleared the company's bank account and absconded to Somalia.

'What are we going to now, Bob?' Valerie said, almost in tears, as they watched the television news about the collapse of the company.

'I'm going straight up to town to see Arkwright, Hislop and Pinder to find out what they propose to do about this financial disaster. I know it's been a nasty shock for you but we must have some sort of redress in this matter. Perhaps we should report the matter to the Financial Ombudsman. Anyway, don't upset yourself. I'll do my best to put things right.'

'I know you will, darling, but we'll not get anything back from the finance company. It's the mining company who lost it or, as it seems, stole it!'

'Don't think about it any more. Go and have a lie down and have a rest until I get back.'

\*\*\*

'I'm sorry sir, but the partners never see anyone without an appointment. Anyway, they are all out today, playing golf,' said the smartly-dressed busty blonde who according to the sign on her office door, was the Personal Assistant to the General Manager.

'Well, Sharon,' Carson said, remembering her name and raising his voice, 'I want to see someone in authority. Is the general manager in?'

'Yes, but Mr Stratton never sees anyone without an appointment.'

The door at the back of the office opened and a portly, red-faced man stood in the doorway. 'What's all the noise about, Sharon?'

'This gentleman wants to see you, but he hasn't got an appointment.'

'Then check the office diary and make one,' Stratton snapped back.

Carson sprang forward, pushed Stratton back into his office and slammed the door shut.

'What I want to know from you is what is your company going to do about my investment!' he thundered.

'How dare you barge your way into my office?' spluttered Stratton.

'Never mind all that, Stratton. I want answers about what happened to my fifty thousand pounds!'

'I don't even know what investment you are talking about, so how can I discuss the matter?'

'It's your scamming copper mining company I'm talking about!'

'Oh, that. Yes that was a very unfortunate turn of events. We've had quite a few investors complaining about it to us, but we can't do anything about it. The funds we passed over to them have been wasted or misappropriated by the chief executive officer and his cronies.'

'So that's it then, is it? You're just going to sit there with your thumb up your arse and do nothing! Can't you get onto the Democratic Republic of Congo to have them arrested and the money paid back to your company?'

'No, I'm afraid that would prove fruitless. Anyway, the people concerned have fled to Somalia for sanctuary. By the way, what is your name and address? I shall need them to enable me to let you know, should we receive any news about the company. We have several hundred investors in the same position as you to pass on any information we may receive, but I doubt we shall hear much more from the Linduana Copper Mining Company.'

'My name is Robert Carson and I intend taking the matter up with the Financial Ombudsman, who will no doubt be looking into your dubious business practices.'

'You'll be wasting your time,' replied Stratton with a smirk. 'There's nothing wrong with our business practices. You invested in the wrong company and there are scores of other investors who've lost a lot more than you.'

'Yes, but I invested on the advice of your company, so I expect you to do something about recovering the misappropriated funds. If you don't I'll have to take what action is open to me!'

Stratton gave a low laugh. 'There's no action open to you except to put it down to your lack of experience in making investments. When it comes to investing in the stock market you are an ill-informed novice. My advice to you is to refrain from making any further investments until you have a better knowledge of the workings of the stock market. Now leave my office. Or I shall call the police?'

'I'm leaving, Stratton, but you can be sure you've not heard the last from me,' Carson said as he slammed the door. He walked out of the office and into the secretary's office. Sharon was absent, probably in the toilet, or taking advantage of her boss being engaged to take a break.

\*\*\*

When Carson arrived home he found Valerie lying on the bed sobbing.

'What's the matter darling? I suppose it's the money, I'm so sorry. I'm afraid my visit was rather a waste of time. But getting upset about it won't change anything.'

'What's upset me is a telephone call I had from Janice when you were out.'

'Why, what did she say?'

'Ben has had an accident. He broke both his legs and injured his back when he fell off the bungalow roof.'

'Oh, poor Ben, what damned awful luck!'

Valerie dried her eyes. 'As you'd expect, she was very upset. She said that the doctors told her he won't be able to do any building work for months and if the injury to his spine is not put right he might never be able to do any sort of manual work again.'

'That certainly is bad news, not only for Janice and Ben, but for us. We can say goodbye to the bungalow extension. Ben was going to do most of the work himself. Now that we've lost most of my gratuity, he won't be able to pay the workers. And he can hardly oversee them sitting in a wheelchair.'

'No, Bob, it seems our plans are well and truly thwarted.'

'Yes, I'm afraid it doesn't look like we'll ever get to Australia. I think the best thing we can do now is put it out of our minds until we can save enough to get us there for a visit. I suggest we have a drink or two and watch something on television to take our minds off our problems.'

'Yes, Bob, that might help me to get to sleep tonight.'

After drinking several brandies while watching a depressing late-night film, they retired.

During the night Valerie was very restless and kept Bob awake. 'I'm sorry, Bob, I can't get to sleep thinking about Ben's accident and how it will affect Janice and the twins. I have a headache. I feel parched. Would you get me a glass of water and an aspirin?'

'Of course, darling,' Bob said, climbing out of bed to go to the kitchen. He returned within two or three minutes to see Valerie threshing about in the bed. He turned on the main light. The bedclothes were flung back and Valerie seemed to be having difficulty breathing.

Bob handed her the glass of water and the aspirin. She dropped them both. She tried to sit up but slipped back helpless, her face sagging oddly.

Bob, my chest! I feel so d-dizzy,' she slurred. She hardly seemed able to speak. Bob realised with horror that his wife must be having a stroke.

'Darling, try to smile!' he said.

Valerie half turned to him; her face drooped to the left.

'Try to raise your arms,' Bob said, now almost certain that she was having a stroke. Valerie raised her right arm and tried to raise her left, but it dropped down to her side. She was lapsing into unconsciousness.

Bob grabbed the bedside telephone and hurriedly dialled 999.

'What is the emergency, police, fire, or ambulance?' A calm voice said.

'I need an ambulance! My wife is having a stroke please hurry! My name is Robert Carson and our address is 20 Phoenix Road, Romford.'

'Please stay calm, sir. A paramedics team should be with you in a few minutes.'

Bob took Valerie's right hand and held it, stroking her brow. She didn't speak, and her eyes seemed sightless. He must get dressed so that he could go to the hospital with her.

The doorbell rang as he was putting on his shoes. He glanced at the bedside clock and saw that twenty minutes had passed since he'd made the call. He hurried to the door and admitted two paramedics, a man and a woman, carrying an assortment of medical equipment. He led them into the bedroom.

The woman quickly examined Valerie and then slowly turned to face Carson. 'I'm very sorry to have to tell you, sir, but your wife has had a serious stroke and we need to get her to the hospital stroke unit immediately.'

The two paramedics wrapped Valerie in a blanket and carried her down the flight of stairs and out of the house to where their ambulance was parked. Carson locked the front door and followed them to the ambulance. The paramedics placed the motionless Valerie on a stretcher. The woman sat beside her and the man climbed into the ambulance and prepared to drive away.

'I haven't got a car, may I join her in the ambulance?' Carson said in a plaintive voice.

The woman gave him a gentle smile and said, 'Of course you can, but please don't disturb your wife.'

Carson climbed into the ambulance and sat on a stretcher opposite Valerie. His gaze was fixed on her motionless figure. Her eyes were closed and her breathing was laboured. He didn't speak to the paramedic, but silently prayed for the ambulance to go faster.

Immediately they arrived at the hospital a waiting group of medical staff sprang into action and Valerie was hurriedly whisked away down passages to the stroke unit. Carson followed, but was told to wait outside the unit. He sat on a bench with his head in his hands, silently praying for Valerie's recovery.

A few minutes later the door of the unit opened and a white-coated, serious-faced doctor came out of the room. Carson stood up and faced the doctor. 'How is she, doctor?'

The doctor cleared his throat before he answered. 'I'm very sorry to have to tell you, Mr Carson, it was too late to save your wife.'

Carson's face blanched. 'You're saying she's dead? Was there nothing you could do to save her?' he implored.

'No, I'm sorry. There wasn't. We did all we could in the short time that she was with us, but your wife had suffered a tremendous stroke, which caused her to have a fatal heart attack.'

'I want to see her, doctor,' Carson said, his mind in a turmoil. He pushed past the doctor to enter the room. He went to Valerie's bedside and sat in a chair and looked down at her still form.

During his life Carson had stoically and almost emotionlessly witnessed the death of many soldiers on battlefields or in makeshift army field hospitals, but the sudden death of his beloved wife was the greatest shock he had ever experienced. 'Someone will pay for this' he muttered to himself, as he walked out of the hospital to catch a late night taxi home.

Back home, he checked the time and worked out that it would be early afternoon in Australia. He made the call he had dreaded. Janice answered the phone.

'I have some very bad news, Janice. Brace yourself for a

shock; your mother has died. She had a stroke followed by a heart attack. I was with her at the end.'

It was almost a full minute before Janice replied. 'Mum's died? It's unbelievable! She was so fit and energetic and never seemed to suffer any problems with her health. We were all looking forward to you both coming out here to live. Ben and the twins will be as heartbroken as I am. I do feel so sorry for you, Dad, with all that's happened to you since you came out of the army.'

'Yes, things are not happening as we had hoped. I'll have to make the arrangements for the funeral. I do want you to come. If you need any money to make the journey let me know and I'll send you a bank draft to cover your fare. I suppose it would be upsetting for the twins to come. They never met their grandmother, so perhaps there isn't much point.'

'Much as I know I should be there and want to be there, if only to comfort you, Dad, I couldn't leave Ben. He needs my constant attention and in his present condition he wouldn't be able to cope with the children. Couldn't you come out here after the funeral and stay with us for a few weeks, until you've decided what you're going to do now that you are alone?'

'Yes, I'd really like to do that, but I have a few matters to attend to before I go anywhere. I'll keep in touch. Give my love to the twins and tell them their granddad will be coming out to see them, as soon as he can. Goodbye, Janice.'

'Make it soon, Dad, I love you,' Janice answered, in a voice that Carson knew would be followed by tears.

# CHAPTER FIVE

Valerie Carson's funeral was held a week later. It was attended by Carson's former commanding officer and a large number of officers, other ranks and their wives, who had known and respected Valerie for her work as the Chair of the Army Wives' Club.

Apart from Janice and the twins, Carson had no living relatives and Valerie's only relatives, a brother and his wife, were living and working in Belize and unable to attend.

After the funeral, when most of the guests had departed the scene, a few of the warrant officers and senior NCOs persuaded Carson to accompany them to the British Legion Club, where they hoped they might help their former RSM to briefly forget his unhappy thoughts. Carson had other things on his mind and didn't want to go, but he appreciated what they were trying to do and agreed.

After all the words of condolence had been said and a couple of rounds of drinks had been drunk, the conversation turned to what Carson had in mind for the future.

'I still intend to make it to Australia,' he said. 'I haven't seen my daughter for five years, and I have never seen my grandchildren, and they are now four years old.'

'What do you plan to do with your time now, Bob?' asked one of the company sergeant majors.

'It'll all have to be put on hold. Valerie's death has rather knocked the stuffing out of me. I'll need to get over that before I think of doing anything, Jack.'

'It might be a good idea for you to travel the country to see all the places in the UK which you've never been able to visit because of all those overseas tours,' a staff sergeant suggested.

'Yes, Harry, I might just do that and call on old members of the regiment,' Carson replied, thinking that that was the last thing he would be doing.

Other members of the group continued to offer advice to Carson about what he could do to occupy his time. He was thankful when the subject was exhausted and conversation turned to recounting tales of the campaigns in which the regiment had been engaged.

As evening approached, the group began to disperse. Carson was alone at the bar chatting with Charlie the barman and about to order one for the road for himself and the Charlie when they were joined by Roger Hurst.

'Put your money away, Sergeant Major, this round is on me,' Hurst said as he climbed onto a bar stool next to Carson.

Why not, thought Carson, who was mellowed by the large number of brandies he had drunk that day. He felt rather sorry for the man. He seemed friendless and nobody in the group that had been in the club earlier had spoken to him or encouraged him to join in their conversations.

'Thank you, Roger, make mine a brandy,' Carson replied, in a voice that betrayed his relaxed mood.

'A half of bitter will do me.' Charlie said. He hadn't much time for Hurst, but he didn't want to make it too obvious in the presence of Carson.

'I heard your wife had died, sir,' said Hurst. 'I guess that's a pretty awful thing to happen at any time, but with your wife being so young and you planning a happy future together in your retirement, that must be as bad as it can get.' He was making his best effort to sound sympathetic.

Carson sipped his brandy before he replied. 'Yes, it's about the worst thing that has happened to me. But if you don't mind I'd rather not talk about it now.'

'I'm sorry, sir, please forgive me, I should have known better,' Hurst said in an obsequious tone.

'Yes, you're forgiven Roger, and you can drop all the 'sirs' and the sergeant major boot-licking' patter. We're both out of the army now and I'm plain Mr Carson, to those who don't know me, and I'll answer to Bob from those who do.' Carson downed his brandy.

'I wasn't prying into your affairs, Bob, but I couldn't help overhearing about all the bad luck you've been having since you left the army. I was wondering if there was anything I could do for you that might improve your lot.'

Carson gave a humourless laugh. 'There's bugger all anyone can do for me. Valerie and I were planning to emigrate to Australia and live with my daughter and grandchildren. My son-in-law was going to build us an extension to his bungalow, but that's not going to happen, because he's had a serious accident and won't be building anything. Then to cap everything else, some damned scamming investment company has managed to con me into investing fifty grand of my gratuity into to some half-arsed copper mining company whose boss and his cronies have buggered off to Somalia with my money.'

'Bloody hell, what rotten luck! Is there nothing you can do?'

'No, I tried the Financial Ombudsman without success. If I could get into Somalia with a gun I'd go after those money-grabbing bastards!'

'Bloody hell, Bob, after hearing all that I think we need another drink. Charlie, make it a large brandy for Bob and a double whisky for me.'

'You'll have to make this your last drink, Mr Hurst, it's past closing time,' Charlie said as he poured the drinks.

'Never mind all that, Charlie, join us with the last drink, and keep the change,' Hurst said as he dropped a twenty-pound note on the bar.

'Now, getting back to what we were talking about, Bob, what's the name of that swindling firm who lost your money?'

Carson pulled his wallet out of his jacket pocket and took out the card that Rackman had given him. 'This is them, and the worst of the bunch is Lance Rackman, their financial consultant. He's a smarmy looking Errol-Flynn type, who I suspect fancies himself as a bit of a lady-killer.' He threw the card onto the bar. Hurst picked it up and read it before slipping it into the top pocket of his jacket.

'I didn't tell you to keep it. What do you want it for?'

'Just in case I decide to invest any money, I want to make sure I steer clear of this shower,' Hurst said with a laugh. He took it out of his pocket, looked at it again and then passed it back to Carson.

'We've certainly had enough to drink, and I don't want Charlie to get in any trouble for keeping the bar open after time, so I suggest we finish our drinks and leave,' Carson said and drained his glass.

Hurst followed suit. 'I'll ring for a taxi and get him to drop you off first,' he said, taking out his mobile phone.

'I'm much obliged, Roger.'

The dispatcher said the taxi would be outside the club in five minutes. They exchanged goodnights with Charlie, and went outside to wait for it.

# CHAPTER SIX

It was 11.15 on a Sunday night in October, and Lance Rackman was sitting in his luxury two-bedroom bungalow in Blackheath Village, South East London. His top-of-the-range music centre was playing Frank Sinatra's top hits.

He was about to pour his fifth double malt whisky of the evening when he was disturbed by the ringing of the doorbell.

'Who the bloody hell is calling at this time of the night?' he muttered as he rose from his reclining armchair. He tied his silk dressing gown cord and went to the front door. He switched the passage light on and opened the front door to see an elderly looking, grey-bearded man. The man was wearing a long raincoat and a cloth cap, which shielded his bespectacled face. A black woollen scarf partially covered the lower part of his face.

'Well, what do you want at this time of night?' snapped Rackman.

'I really am sorry to disturb you so late at night, but you are Mr Lance Rackman, who works for the stockbroker firm of Arkwright, Hislop and Pinder, aren't you? If you are I have urgent need to seek your specialist advice regarding...'

'Yes, I am!' Rackman interrupted with a snarl, 'but why are you calling at my home? I have an office in the city, where I interview prospective clients.'

'Yes, I know where your company offices are, but you have been highly recommended to me and I wanted to make sure that I saw you in person to discuss my plans to make a considerable investment with your company.'

Rackman looked hard at the man. He certainly didn't look as though he would have the capital to make a very large investment, but he might be one of those eccentric old men who had more money than they knew what to do with. It might be worth hearing what he had to say. It could lead to him receiving a substantial commission.

'Then, in the circumstances, sir, I'll be pleased to hear what you propose,' Rackman said with a disarming smile. 'By the way, what is your name?'

'Jack Kilroy,' the man replied as he stepped into the passageway. Rackman closed the door and led him into the sitting room.

As Rackman entered the room, the man withdrew a lead-weighted cosh from his raincoat pocket and struck Rackman a vicious blow on the back of his head. Rackman slumped unconscious to the floor.

Returning his cosh to his pocket, the man took out a pair of surgical gloves and put them on. He then went to the kitchen and took a razor-sharp carving knife from the knife rack. Returning to the sitting room, he plunged the knife into Rackman's chest. He waited a few seconds, then checked Rackman's life signs. There were none.

The man went to a bureau, opened it and looked through its contents before selecting a document, which he put in his pocket. He then scattered the remaining papers over the floor. Next he went into the main bedroom and opened the chest of drawers from the bottom drawer up and scattered the contents over the floor. He did the same in the second bedroom.

Returning to the sitting room, he removed Rackman's gold Rolex watch from his left wrist and a diamond ring from the small finger of his right hand. Leaving the lights on and music centre playing Sinatra's *This is a lovely way to spend an evening, can't think of anything else I'd rather do,* he went to the front door and looked out onto the street. No one was near the bungalow and there was little traffic on the road. He gave the doorbell a quick rub with his scarf, then slipped out onto the pavement and disappeared into the night.

# CHAPTER SEVEN

Mrs Martha Pomeroy unlocked the front door of Lance Rackman's bungalow at 9 am the next day, Monday. It was a practice that had been in place since she had started working for Rackman. He left before she arrived, and she rarely saw him unless he was working from home or taking time off from work.

Martha didn't like Rackman. She thought he was what she would call "a bit of a horny young ram", who fancied his chances with any woman and couldn't keep his trousers zipped up. The proof of her belief was the items of women's underclothing, the state of the bed sheets and the condoms in the lavatory pan she often found on Monday mornings. But he paid her well and always left her weekly wages, together with any instructions to do with his laundry or items of shopping he wanted from the local supermarket, in an envelope on the hall table.

She went to the hall table, but there was no envelope

there. Perhaps he had had one of his boozy nights and forgotten her wages.

She went to the sitting room, where the first thing she saw was the blood-covered body of Rackman, with what she recognized as one of his carving knives stuck in his chest. She screamed involuntarily and, skirting his body, slumped into an armchair. Breathing heavily, she reached into her handbag and took out her mobile phone. She tapped in 999 and a strong but calm voice said, 'What is your emergency?'

'I... I... I've just come to work and found Mr Rackman dead on the floor,' she said in a quavering voice.

'Who's Mr Rackman, who are you and from where are you speaking?'

'My name is Martha Pomeroy, I'm Mr Rackman's housekeeper. I think he's dead and he's got a carving knife stuck in his chest. The address is 23 Sunnydene Avenue, Blackheath.'

'Stay calm, Martha, and remain in the house, but don't touch anything. A team of police officers will be with you in a few minutes.'

It was about 45 minutes before the doorbell rang. Martha tried to avoid looking at Rackman as she went to answer the door. She opened the door and a group of about ten uniformed and plain clothes police officers, led by a plain-clothes man, surged into the hall. The leader produced a warrant card and announced in a loud voice, 'I'm Detective Inspector Ahmed and these are all police officers. Where's the body?'

'In the sitting room,' replied Martha and led the group in.

'Tracey, take Martha into another room and stay with

her while we do the necessary here,' Ahmed said to a uniformed female constable.

'I'm glad to leave the room and the sight of Mr. Rackman's body,' Martha said to Tracey. 'We could go into the spare bedroom.'

Tracey nodded agreement and Martha led her into the bedroom. They sat on the bed. Tracey took a notebook and biro from her shoulder bag.

'I'd like you to tell me exactly what you saw when you first entered the bungalow, Martha,' she said. 'Do you feel up to it now?'

'Yes, I suppose so, if that's what has to be done.'

'I'll take down what you say and then have a statement typed up for you to sign later on. Are you all right with that?'

Martha nodded and related what she had seen when she had entered the bungalow.

The doorbell rang again, and was opened by one of the constables to admit a doctor. In the sitting room, Detective Inspector Ahmed watched the doctor as he carried out his examination. 'There's not much doubt as to what caused his death is there, doc?'

'No, the knife has pierced his heart, but we can't be absolutely sure until an autopsy has been performed. He's also got a nasty lump on the back of his head. That might have killed him, but I suspect he was struck down first and then stabbed.'

'Yeah, certainly looks that way. If you've finished with him, doc, I'll get the coroner's officer to take him to the hospital.'

'Yes, I've done with him, Inspector,' the doctor said as he closed his bag and left the room.

Detective Sergeant Paul Logan approached Ahmed. 'Did you notice that the victim isn't wearing a watch, sir?'

'Yes, the white patch on his wrist between his tanned arm and hand was a clear indication that he was used to wearing one. There was a similar small patch of white skin on the small finger of his right hand. Let's have a word with the housekeeper, she should know if he wore a watch and ring. Bring her in here.'

DS Logan went into the spare bedroom and returned with Martha and Tracey.

'Please sit down, Martha,' Logan said, pointing to the sofa. Noting her shaking hands as she sat down, Logan smiled and said, 'You've nothing to worry about, love. I just need to ask you a few questions.'

Martha relaxed and folded her arms across her chest.

'Did Mr Rackman wear a watch and a ring, Martha?'

'Oh, yes he did. It was a gold Rolex, which he seemed very proud of, and he had a gold ring with a big diamond, which he wore on his little finger.'

Logan gave her an encouraging smile. 'That's very helpful, Martha. Tell me, did anyone else live here? Did he get any friends or other visitors calling?'

'No, nobody else has lived here since I started working for him, but he did get women staying here at weekends.'

'You don't work here at weekends do you, Martha?'

'No, I work from nine to twelve, Monday to Friday.'

'So you haven't seen any of the women who spend weekends here.'

'No, but they leave things behind,' Martha replied. Her worried look returned.

'What sort of things do they leave behind?'

'Bits and pieces of clothing, and I find odd items of make-up on the dressing table in Mr Rackman's bedroom.'

'So, women stayed here and presumably shared Mr Rackman's bed.'

Martha face reddened. 'Yes, they did. Monday is laundry day and I wash all of Mr Rackman's dirty clothes and his bed linen. That's always in a right messy state!'

'It appears to me that you don't approve of his lifestyle.'

'I certainly don't, but he pays well above the minimum pay rate and I live quite near here and walk to work, so I don't have any bus fares to pay.'

Logan gave her a warm smile. 'Just one more question, Martha. Have you ever seen anyone hanging about near the bungalow?'

Martha ran her fingers through her lank hair before she answered. 'Not that I'm aware, but we have had charity people calling for clothing.'

'Thank you, Martha, you've been most helpful. You can go home now, but we may need to see you again, so let PC Wyatt have your address and phone number before you leave.'

'I've already got Mrs Pomeroy's details, Sarge,' interposed Tracey, who was ambitious and always eager to show that she was on the case and taking care of business. 'I also took a statement from her while we were in the bedroom.'

Logan, who was used to her self-promoting style, smiled and said, 'Thank you Tracey. Let DS Lord have Mrs Pomeroy's statement.'

As Mrs Pomeroy let herself out of the bungalow, a tall, grey-haired man stood outside the door. 'I'm Detective Chief

Inspector Owen Warner,' he said as he passed his warrant card in front of her face, 'Who are you?'

'I'm Mrs Martha Pomeroy, Mr Rackman's housekeeper,' she said, as she made to close the door behind her.

'Leave the door, I'm going in. Have you been released by DI Ahmed?'

'Yes, I was told I could go home.'

'That's OK, then, but I may need to see you some time in the future,' Warner said as he entered the bungalow.

'So, what's afoot, Ahmed?' Warner jibed as he approached Ahmed.

'Twelve inches, guv, or if you're metrically-minded, approximately 30 centimetres.'

'OK, Ahmed, that's enough of the Holmes and Watson banter. I see you've had the body taken away. Who was he, and how was he killed?'

'The doctor reckoned the victim, a Mr Lance Rackman, died from a stab wound to the heart with a kitchen knife. The housekeeper, Mrs Martha Pomeroy, identified the knife as belonging to the knife rack in the kitchen. The doctor also found a nasty bruise on the back of Rackman's head, which he said could have caused his death. Of course we won't get a final report until the body's been examined by a pathologist.'

Warner nodded agreement. 'I met the housekeeper as I came in. Was she able to give you anything useful?'

'She said the victim's gold Rolex watch and diamond ring were missing.'

'So, judging by the papers that have been taken from the bureau, it looks as though the house was burgled.'

'Yes, and the bedrooms have also been ransacked. But

what I find rather strange is that if the burglar had knocked Rackman senseless, why did he kill him?'

'Warner nodded. 'You're beginning to agree with what I've been thinking. Have all the windows and doors been checked for signs of a break-in?'

'Yes, of course, and nothing was found that indicated one.'

'So our killer must have either had a key to the front door or was let in by the victim.'

'Yes, but the doctor put the time of death at about midnight, or a little before,' said Logan. 'Rather late for a visitor, and Mrs Pomeroy has stated that he never got any visitors apart from young women who sometimes stayed for dirty weekends.'

'Hmm, I think it's unlikely that one of his lady friends killed him. The blow on his head, the knife through his heart and the appearance of a burglary suggest to me that this was a planned killing and that the theft of the watch and the ring and emptying of drawers were simply an effort to make it look as though it had been a burglary. Have the SOCO team found anything of interest?'

Ahmed shook his head. 'Not up to now. They've lifted fingerprints, most of which belong to the victim, but they've not found anything that could help identify the killer.'

'Keep them at it, Ahmed. Remember, intruders always leave a trace of their presence at the crime scene.'

'That's something I learned when I first became a detective,' Ahmed replied with a wide grin.

'What do we know about the victim? Was he married? Has he any relatives in the area? What was his job? We'll need someone to formally identify him.'

'Mrs Pomeroy could do that. She did tell us that he didn't seem to have any family or friends that called, but ladies of the night often stayed here at weekends.'

'But apart from his killer, he apparently didn't have company last night. Get a couple of your team to call on neighbours to see if any of his lady callers can be identified. One of them might be his killer. Your next move should be to interview his boss, whoever he is, and see if he can throw any light on Rackman's relationships and business dealings. They might have had some bearing on his death.'

'From documents I found in his bureau, it seems he was a financial consultant for a firm of stockbrokers called Arkwright, Hislop and Pinder. They have offices in Threadneedle Street.'

'Good, then away you go and take DC Benson with you. She needs the experience.'

# CHAPTER EIGHT

'There are two detectives in my office who want to see you, Mr Stratton,' Sharon Tate, his PA, said on the office intercom.

'Have they identified themselves?' Stratton replied.

'Oh yes, Mr Stratton, they've shown me their warrant cards.'

'Then bring them in.'

Sharon opened his door and led the two detectives into the office. 'This is Detective Inspector Ahmed and Detective Constable Benson,' Sharon said, and turned to leave the office.

'Please remain, Sharon, I might need you to take notes.'

Sharon sat in a chair next to Stratton.

Stratton rose from his desk and approached Ahmed and Benson. 'What can I do for you, Inspector?'

'We have some rather unpleasant news for you, sir,' Ahmed said.

'Then please be seated and tell me,' Stratton said, pointing to a settee against the side wall. Ahmed and Benson sat down. Benson took a notebook and pen from her handbag.

'Have you an employee named Lance Rackman, sir?'

'Yes, he's our top financial consultant. He's not in any trouble is he?'

'I'm sorry to say he was found dead in his home this morning, by his housekeeper.'

Stratton paled and Sharon let out a loud 'Oh!'

'My god! How did he die? He always seemed as fit as a fiddle,' Stratton said.

'He was murdered, sir.'

'No! Have you caught his killer?'

'No, not yet. It seems likely that he was the victim of a burglar, but this is in some doubt and under close investigation. I'm hoping you might be able to give us information about his background and any details about his family, friends and associates.'

Stratton gazed up at the ceiling, deep in thought. 'All I can tell you is that he was unmarried and as far as I'm aware he had no relatives. I don't know of any friends he might have had. His only associates in this company are two other consultants, Keith Dawlish and Hugh Fry, our three principals, Albert Arkwright, Desmond Hislop, George Pinder and, of course, Sharon and me.'

'Are any of your principals available for interview?'

'No, I'm afraid not. They are all away on a three-week golfing holiday in Portugal.'

'What about your consultants, Dawlish and Fry?'

'They work from home. I expect they will be out visiting some of our prospective investors. Anyway, I doubt that any of them would be able to give you any more information about Lance Rackman than I have. He didn't have much contact with them. He reported directly to me. If you wish to interview any of those I have mentioned, Sharon can let you have their phone numbers and addresses.'

'Yes, I'd like to have those.'

'OK. Sharon, let Inspector Ahmed have what he wants before he leaves.'

Sharon rose to leave the office.

'Before you go Miss Tate, I have a few questions for you. It is Miss, isn't it?

'No, I prefer Ms,' she said and sat down.

Ahmed nodded at DC Benson. 'Over to you, Tamara.'

Benson cleared her throat. 'Can you tell us anything about Mr Rackman, Sharon?'

Sharon reddened slightly and looked embarrassed. 'I thought he was a bit familiar, and he was always pestering me to go to his home or take me out for meals, the cinema or the theatre. He's thirty-eight, ten years older than me and not my type at all.'

'You never mentioned any of this to me, Sharon,' Stratton interposed. 'If I'd known I would have told him to desist from that sort of behaviour.'

'Well, I knew how you and everyone else thought what a marvellous salesman he was. I didn't want to be the cause of any upset.'

'Do you know about any of Mr Rackman's lady friends?' Benson said.

'No, I have no knowledge about any of them and if he did have any, I should think their relationships wouldn't last very long.'

'OK, Tamara, I'll take it from here,' Ahmed said. He turned to Stratton. 'Just one more question for you, sir. In your recent experience, has Rackman had any problems with disgruntled clients?'

'Well... er... that is possible. The company has recently suffered a great disappointment over an investment Rackman had arranged with a copper mining company in Congo. The company collapsed and our shareholders lost thousands of pounds. Naturally, they weren't too happy. To make matters worse the chief executive of the copper company ran off to Somalia with the rest of the money that had been invested with them. As you might imagine we've had quite a lot of angry investors expecting us to take some action to recover the stolen money. Of course, there's little we can do about that.'

'Hmm. This seems to throw a new light on what might have happened to your Mr Rackman. Are you aware of any your shareholders having threatened him?'

'No, but Sharon can let you have a complete list of all the shareholders who have complained and threatened us with all types of action, which thankfully, would have proved quite fruitless.'

'That would be very helpful, sir. However, it is quite possible that I might have further questions to ask you in the future.'

Stratton looked relieved. 'Sharon, let Detective Inspector Ahmed have all the information on your computer on the Linduana Copper Mining Company and the staff telephone numbers and addresses.'

Sharon led Ahmed and Benson into her office and sat at her computer to download the information required.

# CHAPTER NINE

DCI Warner and DI Ahmed met up with their superior officer, Detective Superintendent Ralph Braddock, early the following morning.

'Well, what have you learned so far about this Rackman bloke?' asked Braddock.

'Quite a lot, but nothing that points to his killer,' said Warner. 'Ahmed and I have prepared a report. It gives a summary of what we've got from the people we've interviewed so far.' He drew a sheaf of papers from his briefcase and placed them on the superintendent's desk.

Braddock picked up the report and gave it a cursory glance. 'I'll read this later,' he said, dropping it into his pending tray. 'But I'd like to hear what theories you may have formed from your enquiries.'

Warner turned to Ahmed. 'You were first on the scene. You'd better give the boss what you saw and any ideas you have about what happened.'

Ahmed sat up straight in his chair and cleared his throat. 'As soon as the call came in I took a SOCO team and other officers from the duty shift. We learnt from the victim's housekeeper, Mrs Martha Pomeroy, that she had arrived at 9 am and found her employer, Lance Rackman, dead in the sitting room with a carving knife stuck into his chest. She identified the knife as one belonging to the rack in the kitchen. From the disarray seen in the sitting room and the two bedrooms, coupled with the fact that Rackman's wristwatch, a gold Rolex, and a diamond ring had been removed from him, it appeared to have been a burglary. The doctor found that Rackman had sustained a blow on the back of his head, which, he thought, might possibly have killed him, or at least rendered him unconscious. However he considered that the stabbing was probably the cause of his death. We should know later today, as a post mortem is being carried out this morning.'

'Were there any signs of a break in?' Braddock interposed.

'No, we made a thorough check and found nothing, sir.'

'Then that suggests to me that Rackman admitted someone to his home and was rendered unconscious by his guest, who then carried out what was supposed to be a burglary and stabbed him to death with one of his own knives. This looks to me to have been a murder by someone known to Rackman.'

'That's exactly what I thought, sir,' Warner said.

Ahmed looked questioningly at Warner. 'Shall I carry on, guv?'

'Yes, please do, Samier.'

'We learned from Mrs Pomeroy that apart from various

young women who stayed at the bungalow over the weekend, as far as she was aware Rackman had no other callers. I visited his employer, who informed me that as far as he knew Rackman was unmarried and had no known family or friends. I am arranging to call on all of Rackman's colleagues to find out if they have any other information about Rackman's personal life.'

'Yes, Samier, I agree with that course of action. It might also be worthwhile to arrange house-to-house calls on his neighbours to see if any of them can identify any of his lady visitors.'

'I've already done that, sir.'

'Good! Away you go then and let me know if your enquiries provide anything that might suggest a motive for this murder.' Braddock dismissed them with a wave of his hand.

# CHAPTER TEN

Carson washed and dried the day's used utensils and crockery and put them away neatly in the kitchen cabinet. He liked everything to be kept in an orderly manner. He had learned that lesson during his early army service, and had ensured that the soldiers in his battalion maintained the high standards he set.

What to do now? He'd written to his daughter and the letter was waiting on the hall table to be posted. He picked up a mystery novel he had bought that morning, but his mind was too preoccupied by real-life problems to allow him to concentrate on reading.

He switched on the television to catch the evening news. The first item he saw was a reporter interviewing a detective chief inspector named Warner, who was appealing to the public for information regarding Lance Rackman, who had been found dead in his bungalow. The reporter was trying to elicit more than the detective seemed willing to impart. The detective's closing remark was: 'All I can say at this time is that Mr Rackman appears to have been the victim of an attack by a burglar. The investigation is continuing and...'

Carson smiled grimly as he switched off the television. Rackman couldn't be a more deserving murder victim. 'I'll have a drink to that,' he mused as he reached for his bottle of brandy.

# CHAPTER ELEVEN

DI Ahmed and his section of detectives were sitting in DCI Warner's office for a briefing.

'I want you and DS Lord to call on Keith Dawlish and see if you can learn anything about his former investment colleague, the late Lance Rackman,' said Warner. 'I've telephoned Dawlish and he'll be at home this afternoon. His address is in this case file.' He passed the file across his desk to Ahmed.

'OK, boss, we'll leave straight after our lunch break,' replied Ahmed. 'What about the other consultant, Hugh Fry? Do you want us to see him too?'

'No, DS Logan and I will call on him. He'll be at his home this afternoon. When we've done we'll meet up here and talk about what we've found out. The rest of your troops can spend time doing a thorough search of Rackman's bungalow for anything that might help to identify any of the women who have stayed with him. There's just a chance that one of them may have killed him. Uniform have made house-to-house calls on his neighbours, but they didn't learn anything of value when they called during the daytime. Evening calls might catch more at home.'

\*\*\*

'This is Keith Dawlish's address, Debra - stop here,' said Ahmed.

DS Debra Lord braked their car opposite a three-storey block of flats.

'He's in Flat 1 on the ground floor,' said Ahmed, as they got out of the car.

They climbed the three steps to the front door and Lord pressed the doorbell. A few seconds passed and then the door was opened by a tall, pale-faced, bearded man of around forty, who was dressed in jeans and a check sports shirt.

'Mr Dawlish? I'm Detective Inspector Ahmed and my colleague is Detective Sergeant Lord,' said Ahmed as he flashed his warrant card in front of Dawlish.

'Yes, I was expecting you, Inspector, DCI Warner rang me this morning. Come in,' replied Dawlish. He opened the door wider and led them into his sitting room.

The walls of the room were covered with bookcases which were filled, haphazardly, with books of all shapes and sizes. A computer desk, holding a laptop and a clutter of files and papers, was under the window. The only furniture was a large leather chesterfield, two small easy chairs and a glass-topped occasional table. There was a strong smell of coffee coming through the open door to the kitchen.

'Please take a seat,' Dawlish said, indicating the two easy chairs. 'I've just made some coffee, would you like some?'

'No thanks, sir, we won't take up too much of your time,' said Ahmed. 'We're just here to ask you a few questions about your colleague, Lance Rackman. You'll have heard he was found dead in his home on Monday morning.' He sat down in one of the easy chairs. Lord followed suit and took her pocket book and a pen from her handbag.

'Yes, what a dreadful occurrence,' said Dawlish with a little shudder. 'He was stabbed, I believe.'

Ahmed nodded. 'How long have you known Rackman?'

Dawlish ran his fingers through his tousled hair before he answered. 'Oh, about eight years. I joined the company ten years ago and Rackman joined a couple of years later.'

'Were you both employed as financial consultants?'

'Yes, we and a fellow colleague, Hugh Fry, were a three-man team, employed to give investment advice to potential investors.'

'How did you get along with Rackman?'

Dawlish's lips tightened before he replied. 'Not very well, I'm afraid.'

'Was there any particular reason for your differences, sir?'

'Yes, there certainly was. He was an absolute bounder. He was always making snide remarks to Hugh and me. He was also a liar and a cheat and he made a play for every attractive woman he met.'

'So I don't suppose you had much to do with him outside of working hours?'

'No, but I did hear about some his unprofessional dealings with his customers.'

'Such as?'

'To clinch a deal he would always grossly exaggerate the likely profitability of an investment to a potential investor.'

'Surely that practice would not have been acceptable by your directors?'

Dawlish gave a short laugh. 'As long as Rackman made money for the company, and he did make a lot, our directors didn't give a damn how he did it.'

'Was he involved in the sale of shares on behalf of the Linduana Copper Mining Company?'

'He certainly was. Hugh Fry and I warned our general manager that the company was being far too optimistic about its forecast of a high yield of copper, which would have had resulted in a great increase in value of their investments. But he encouraged Rackman to sell all he could. As we anticipated, the company crashed and many of Rackman's clients lost a considerable amount of money.'

'I imagine that caused great disappointment for Rackman's clients,' Ahmed said.

'It certainly did. We had no end of complaints and threats made and lost many clients.'

'Yes, your Mr Stratton gave me a list of your complainants, but are you aware of any particular threats made?'

'No, Hugh and I were not in any way involved with Rackman's balls-up, but some of our long-term investors dropped us.'

'You described Rackman as a being over-familiar with his female clients. Have you any knowledge about any of his personal affairs?'

'No, not really, Inspector. We heard, second hand, a few

complaints from Sharon Tate and a few of our female investors.'

'I've just one more question and then we'll let you get on with your day. What were you doing between the hours of 10 pm and midnight last Sunday?'

Dawlish looked slightly embarrassed before he answered. 'I was here all night.'

'Is there anyone who can verify that?'

'Yes, Hugh Fry was here. We were playing chess.'

'What time did he arrive?'

'Around 9 pm.'

'When did he leave?'

'He didn't leave that night. It was past midnight when we finished our game, so he stayed the night.'

Ahmed rose from his chair. 'Thank you sir, you have been most helpful, but we may want to see you again.'

Lord put her pocket book and pen back into her handbag and stood waiting for Ahmed's next move.

'Please don't trouble yourself, Mr Dawlish, we'll see ourselves out,' Ahmed said.

DS Lord exchanged goodbyes with Dawlish as she followed Ahmed out of the room.

# CHAPTER TWELVE

The following morning DI Ahmed and DS Lord joined DCI Warner and DS Logan in the DCI's office.

'Well, how did your interview go with Keith Dawlish?' Warner asked.

'OK, boss, but nothing to get excited about. Debra has made a report from her pocket book notes and it's in the typing pool.'

'Good. Just give me a verbal resumé of what you found out.'

Ahmed went to great lengths, without interruption from the others, to mention everything that had passed between him and Dawlish.

'What you say matches up well with what we learned from Hugh Fry,' said Warner. 'We thought he was as camp as a row of tents. So it looks like he and Dawlish are gay partners. Much as they both disliked, or even hated Rackman, I think it's unlikely that they had anything to do with his death.'

'So, as far as the employees of Messrs Arkwright, Hislop and Pinder go, we only have Roland Stratton, the company's general manager, and his PA, Sharon Tate, left as possible suspects' said Ahmed. 'The three partners were all in Portugal when Rackman was murdered and they're still out of the country.'

'Yes, so I believe, Ahmed. I'd like you to check when they're coming back and for you and DS Logan to interview them. From what we have learned from Fry and Dawlish the partners are not likely to be too critical of Rackman, as any strong criticism of his dealings with his clients would reflect badly on their management of his work practices.'

'The house-to-house calls on Rackman's neighbours proved fruitless, boss. No one said they'd seen any of Rackman's visitors. He probably arranged for his guests to arrive late in the evening and leave very early in the morning. One resident said there had been a lot of visits from people collecting clothing for various charities.'

'That might be significant. A bogus collection could provide a cover for Rackman's killer doing a recce of Rackman's home. See if you can find out when the last visit was made before Rackman's death,' Warner said.

'Anything else, boss?'

'Yes, you can arrange to interview all the complainants that are on that list that Stratton's PA gave you.'

'Bloody hell, boss there's scores of them!'

'I know, so I suggest you give priority to the investors who lost the most. Oh yes, there's something else you can do. Get one of your DCs to visit all the local jewellers and pawnbrokers to see if Rackman's Rolex and diamond ring have been offered for sale.'

'Don't you think it's more likely that if the killer wasn't a burglar he might be tempted to keep the watch and ring?'

'Yes, Samier, that's a possibility, so when you interview the complainants have a crafty gander at the watch they're wearing. Reflex gold watches are unmistakable!'

'Right, boss if there's nothing else, we'll make a start before you think of something more for us to do,' Ahmed said with a laugh.

'Off you go then, and keep me up to date with anything worth knowing,' Warner said.

# CHAPTER THIRTEEN

'Double brandy please, Charlie,' said Carson as he sat at the bar.

Charlie poured the drink and placed it in front of Carson. 'You're the first customer I've had this evening,' he said.

'Yes, I did notice. Apart from a few darts and pool players, the place is empty.'

'Oh, that lot. They're the usual members who use the club's facilities but never buy a drink,' said Charlie as he placed Carson's change on the bar. 'But that mate of yours comes in most evenings and puts a few drinks away.'

'My mate - who's that?'

'Roger Hurst.'

'I wouldn't describe him as a mate, Charlie.'

'I was only going by the way you two were chatting and drinking together to well past closing time, a couple of weeks ago.'

'Oh, that time. It was after my wife's funeral and I was depressed and felt ready for any company. I probably drank too much to care who it was.'

'Blimey, talk of the devil and he's sure to appear,' said Charlie.

Carson turned to see Hurst, a broad grin on his face, approaching the bar.

'Good evening, Bob. My usual tipple, Charlie,' he said as he sat next to Carson.

'Evening, Roger. How are you?'

Hurst took a gulp of his whisky before he answered. 'I'm fine. I'm glad you're here tonight. I thought you might be celebrating,' he said with a wink.

'Celebrating? I've got nothing to celebrate!'

'Let's sit at a table and talk about it,' said Hurst, picking up his drink and walking across to a table in the corner of the room.

'Excuse us, Charlie,' Carson said. He picked up his drink and followed Hurst. 'Now what's this all about, Roger?'

'Don't you keep up with the news, Bob?'

'Of course, I do. I read the Guardian and watch the BBC news morning and night.'

'Then you must have seen the news report about your financial consultant, Lance Rackman, being murdered by a burglar.'

'Yes, I did catch something about it on the news. I can't say I was sorry to hear it, but his murder is hardly something for me to celebrate. It doesn't get any of my investment money back.'

'You're not jesting with me, are you, Bob?'

'No, of course not! Why should you think that?'

'Because when I first heard about the murder, I thought you might have had something to do with it. Like hiring a hit man to do the job for you,' Hurst said in a low voice.

'If you thought that about me you must be on something very potent. If I did want him dead that much, I'd do it myself. I wouldn't waste what money I have to hire someone else to do my dirty work. Anyway, hiring someone else puts you in their power and leaves you open to blackmail.'

Hurst spread his arms. 'I'm sorry, Bob, I misjudged you. You're quite right in what in what you say. But after the way you were treated by that investment company, I thought you had a good motive for taking some sort of revenge.'

'Hmm… yes, a lot of the investors lost much more than me. One of them could be a psychopathic type who might be vengeful enough to murder him. But if you don't mind, can we leave it at that?'

'Yes, anything you say, Bob. I think we need another drink. Charlie, same again please,' he called across the room.

Charlie brought the drinks to their table. 'Will you be making a night of it? Because as you're the only two here now, I thought I'd close a little earlier.'

'As far as I'm concerned, Charlie, this is my one for the road,' Carson said as he pushed a twenty-pound note into his hand.

'Thanks a lot, sir, sorry, I mean Bob, you're a real gent,' Charlie said and returned to the bar.

Hurst took a quick gulp of his whisky. 'I was going to pay for that round, Bob and that was a very large tip you gave Charlie. He'll be expecting all of us to cough up big tips in future.'

'Nobody has to be obliged to do as I do. I've always rewarded good service and I consider Charlie to be a very deserving case.'

Hurst gave a slight shrug of his shoulders. 'I just thought you'd be counting every penny

after your investment in copper was lost.'

Carson gave a short laugh. 'I'm not on the breadline yet, Roger.'

'That's good. So what about a run up to the Big Smoke this weekend, to see a show or film, followed by a decent meal somewhere?'

Carson rubbed his chin in thought. Why not? Hurst wasn't the type of man he'd choose as a friend, but then he had not been offered any sort of companionship by any of the other members of the club, most of whom were married, or much younger and without his experience of life.

'Well, I don't think I'll get a better offer, so what did you have in mind, Roger?'

'Have you ever seen The Mousetrap?'

'No, I've never spent much time in London to see any shows, but I know it's been running for a very long time.'

'Yes, it's been running in London for sixty years and it's on most people's bucket list. If you're interested I'll book us for Saturday evening and a restaurant for a meal after the show.'

'OK, Roger, you're on. What about the expenses?'

'We can go dutch on the tickets and the meal, if that's all right with you?'

'Yes that's fine. So where do we meet, Roger?'

'Since we're on different lines to London, I suggest we make our way separately to

Charing Cross Station and meet in the bar at the Charing Cross Hotel at about 6 pm. I'll give you my mobile phone number and you give me yours so that we can contact each other if there's any change of plan.'

'Mobile phone? I haven't got one. I suppose I'll have to get one to survive in Civvy Street in the 21st century.'

'Yes, you'll certainly need one.'

'Right, Roger, it's a date then. Now let's finish these drinks and let Charlie close the place. I'll book a cab and arrange to drop you off at your home first.'

# CHAPTER FOURTEEN

It was a little after four o'clock on Saturday afternoon and Roland Stratton had come into his office to check the mail, most of which was letters of complaint from Lance Rackman's former clients. He quickly read through the letters and placed most of them in Sharon Tate's in-tray to be answered with a stock reply on Monday morning. Those which contained threats of legal action he locked in his desk drawer. These would be passed to the company's solicitor.

He locked his office and left the building to walk the short distance to where his car was parked. He opened the door, got in and made ready to drive off. But as he leaned forward to start the engine, a pair of gloved hands reached out from the back seat and lowered a thin cord over his head. Before Stratton realised what was happening, the cord was pulled tight.

Stratton choked and tried to grab the cord, struggling to look around. All he could see in the mirror, with his bulging eyes, were the two gloved hands pulling the cord tighter and tighter. He tried to scream, but no sound came. He struggled violently until he lapsed into unconsciousness.

The assassin removed the cord, took his right-hand glove off and felt for life signs. There were none. He got out of the car and into the front passenger seat. He searched through Stratton's pockets and removed a bunch of keys from his raincoat pocket, then replaced his glove and got out of the car. He walked back to the building Stratton had left and tried the front door; it was locked. He checked Stratton's keys and found the one to open the door.

He entered the building, which was in total darkness. Then he took a small torch from his overcoat pocket and shone it on all the doors as he walked down a short passageway. The last office on the passage was identified as 'Roland Stratton, General Manager'. The door was locked. He checked the keys until he found the right one, then entered. By the light of his torch he could see that this was an outer office, occupied by Stratton's secretary. A wooden plaque fixed to the desk and bearing the name, "Sharon Tate, PA to General Manager" confirmed this.

He crossed the office to another door, which bore Stratton's name. It too was locked. He checked the keys. There were now only two that he had not used, the key that opened Stratton's office and what looked like a safe key. He entered the windowless office and switched on the light. The only furniture was a large desk and swivel chair, two easy chairs, a bookcase with rows of books and a large metal safe in a corner of the office.

He opened the safe, which contained several files marked 'CONFIDENTIAL' and two box files. He opened one of the boxes. It was full of fifty-pound notes in bundles, secured with elastic bands, each amounting to one thousand pounds. He counted the bundles; there were sixty. He opened the other box file. It also contained sixty bundles. He licked his lips and gave a low whistle. What a haul, £120,000!

He took a plastic bin liner from his overcoat pocket and emptied the contents of the two boxes into the bag. Then he placed the boxes in the safe in the position in which he had found them and closed the safe door and locked it. He switched off the office light and left the building, locking the doors that he had unlocked when he had entered the building.

Walking back to the car park, he saw that Stratton's car was as he had left it. The body had not been discovered. He returned Stratton's keys to his jacket pocket. Returning to his car, he placed the plastic bag under the back seat and drove out of the car park into the gathering dusk of the late afternoon.

*\*\**

Carson checked his watch: 1820 hours. He had arrived at the Charing Cross Hotel at 17.50. Every soldier knows you should parade at least five minutes early, so where was Hurst? He would give him another ten minutes, then go.

He had drained his brandy glass and started to put on his raincoat when the door opened and Hurst walked in.

'I'm really sorry to be so late. I missed the train I should have caught to get here on time, so I came by taxi. It's okay though, we've got plenty of time to have a drink before we leave for the theatre. What's yours, the usual brandy?'

Carson nodded and took his raincoat off. Hurst returned from the bar with what Carson estimated to be a triple whisky and a triple brandy.

'Hey, steady on, Roger! I had a double while I was waiting for you.'

'That's all right, Bob, we won't be driving. We'll go home in a black cab, my treat.'

'That'll be a bit pricey for the journey we've got to make,' said Carson.

'Don't give it another thought, Bob, I've had a bit of luck on the gee-gees this week.'

They finished their drinks in silence.

'Well, I suppose we should be off,' said Hurst, glancing at his watch.

Outside the hotel, Hurst said, 'The curtain's raised at 7.30, so we've got 45 minutes to get to the theatre and with this heavy traffic a taxi would take about fifteen minutes to get there. It would be quicker to walk.'

'I'll tell you what, Roger,' said Carson with a broad grin, 'to save time we could march there in double time.'

'Okay, if that's what you want, let's do it.'

They arrived at St Martin's Theatre in less than ten minutes. Hurst produced his tickets and they were shown to the front stalls.

'What do you think about it so far?' said Hurst as they sat in the bar during the intermission.

'Oh, it's quite good, but I can't see why it's run for so long.'

'That's because it has become a must-see for theatre-loving tourists. Some travel companies even include it in their package holiday offers.'

At the sound of the bell to end the intermission, they quickly finished their drinks and returned to their seats to see the second half of the play. Standing in the foyer, Carson said, 'So where have you booked us for dinner, Roger?'

'Oh, it's a place I use quite a lot. It's just around the corner. They've got a very varied menu, so I'm sure you'll find something to your liking.'

'Yes, I'm sure I shall. After forty years of army food, I'm fairly easily satisfied.'

'Since my divorce, I've done my own cooking,' said Hurst. 'My wife walked out on me after I was discharged. It's nothing special, but at least I get to eat what I want.'

Five minutes later they were ordering their meal in the restaurant. Both enjoyed their meal and thirty minutes later they were outside waiting for a taxi.

'You must let me know how much I owe you for all this entertainment and dining,' said Carson.

Hurst gave a little laugh. 'Don't give it another thought, Bob, it was a pleasure to have your company and, as I said, I picked up a few winners this week, which has nicely covered my expenses.'

'Very well, but I insist on paying the taxi fare and next time we get together it'll be my treat,' said Carson.

The taxi dropped Hurst off outside the block of ill-maintained high-rise flats where Hurst lived in North Woolwich.

When he got home, Carson poured a brandy and sat pondering on the evening with Hurst. The only thing they had in common was their army service. Hurst had been a very competent platoon sergeant and had he not ruined his career, he would have progressed to the higher noncommissioned ranks. With hindsight it wasn't too difficult to understand how he had reacted over the loss of two members of his platoon and his inept and brutal handling of a courageous prisoner of war, who despite being beaten until near death would not reveal his unit's position.

# CHAPTER FIFTEEN

The morning briefing over, DCI Warner joined Detective Superintendent Braddock in his office.

'You wished to see me boss, regarding the Rackman case?' said Warner.

'Yes I do, Owen. The Borough Commander has received a call from the Deputy Commissioner, City of London Police, advising that a dead body, identified as that of Roland Stratton, has been found in a car in a parking lot near Threadneedle Street. He is aware that Stratton was the General Manager of the firm in which Rackman was employed and that we are investigating the matter.'

'I suppose that means the investigation is being passed to us,' Warner said.

'Well, it does make it a tidier investigation if we work in one manor. From their initial investigation they've learned that Stratton was strangled from behind, probably by someone who had been hiding in the back of the car.'

'That makes it very much like a premeditated Mafia-type murder, boss.'

'Yes, that's how it occurred to me. I've seen all those Godfather films,' Braddock replied with a short, humourless laugh. 'Anyway, get Ahmed's section to liaise with the City CID to see what else they can learn. It does seem to me to be developing into a case of revenge killings over the loss of investments, caused by the crash of that Linduana copper mining company. So put as many men that can be spared on the case to interview the investors who have made threats to the investment company, or have lost considerable sums of money.'

'Right, boss I'll get right on to it.'

***

Later that day the City of London Police CID faxed their report on the death of Stratton. It contained little more information than the Borough Commander had received by telephone. They also had Stratton's car delivered to the police vehicle compound in Lewisham.

DI Ahmed had the SOCO team make a thorough search of the vehicle's interior for anything that might help to identify Stratton's killer.

'I'm afraid we didn't even come up with a hair on the back seats, guv,' said the SOCO team leader, reporting to Ahmed after the inspection.

Ahmed sent for DS Logan. 'I want you to take your section to that car park near Threadneedle Street and take a note of the registration numbers of all the cars there. Then get the names and addresses of the car owners. They're probably living within a few miles of London and are regular users of that car park. They should then be interviewed to ascertain if they saw anything odd on the day Stratton was murdered. Apparently Stratton died some time between four and six that evening, a time when many people would be leaving their offices to drive home. For example, did they see a car that had not been parked there before, or a man acting suspiciously in any way?'

'That's a tall order, guv.'

'I know Paul, but someone may have seen a man getting into Stratton's car. You might also have a word with the man who reported seeing Stratton dead in his car. The City CID didn't include his name in their report. They simply said that a member of the public who regularly used the car park happened to glance into Stratton's car and saw that he appeared to be dead.'

***

The following morning, DS Logan reported back to DI Ahmed that he and his team had interviewed more than twenty regular users of the car park and none of them could provide any information about Stratton's car or any suspicious persons being in the car park.

'What about the man who reported seeing Stratton dead in his car?' Ahmed asked.

Logan handed Ahmed a slip of paper. 'That's his name and address. We went to his home, but his wife told us that her husband was out of the country on a business trip and was unlikely to be back for several weeks. I had a word with the sergeant who dealt with the report but he was unable to provide anything that was of use to our investigation.'

Ahmed sighed deeply. 'Well, let me have a written report of what you've done for the boss. You can now make a start on visiting all the people who invested in the Linduana Mining Company.'

Logan groaned. 'The trouble with this damned case is that there are too many suspects, guv.'

'Never mind Paul, the extra legwork might help to slim down some of your overweight

officers. If you need any help with your enquiries I'll send DS Lord's section to assist you.'

# CHAPTER SIXTEEN

Carson was opening a tin of salmon for his evening meal when the doorbell rang.

.  'Who the hell can that be?' he muttered as he went to the front door.

He opened the door to see two men in dark suits. The older of the two produced a police warrant card for Carson's inspection, 'I'm DS Logan and this is DC Holt,' he said, indicating his tall young companion, who was holding his warrant card in front of Carson.

'Are you Mr Robert Carson, sir?'

'Yes, I am. What can I do for you, Sergeant?'

'May we come in, sir?'

'Yes, when you've told me what this is all about.'

'We're investigating a double murder, sir,' Logan almost whispered.

'You can come in, but I can't for the life of me understand why you want to interview me about two murders,' Carson said as he opened the door wide to admit them and led them into his sitting room. Carson sat in his favourite armchair. 'Please be seated gentlemen, and tell me what this is all about.'

Logan and Holt sat on the sofa. Logan took a file from his briefcase and Holt took his pocket book and a biro from his pocket.

'We were rather hoping that you would be able to help us with our investigation in the death of a Mr Lance Rackman, who we understand to have dealt with your investment on behalf of the Linduana Copper Mining Company,' Logan said.

'Well, I'm sorry, but I can't be of much help to you, because all I know about Mr Lance Rackman is that he sold me shares in the company you mention. I only saw him on two occasions and I learned recently that he had been killed in his home by a burglar.'

Logan consulted his file before replying. 'I understand that you invested a very large sum with the company he was representing.'

'Yes, it was a large sum, fifty thousand pounds to be exact. It was most of the terminal grant I received on my retirement from the army.'

'Oh, so you were in the army, sir. What regiment did you serve with?'

'The Essex and Hertfordshire Light Infantry, Sergeant, but I don't see that my army service can relate in any way to your enquiries regarding Lance Rackman,' Carson sharply retorted.

Logan smiled and Holt busied himself writing notes. 'I quite agree, sir, but we are required to ask routine questions about a person's background when we are interviewing the person in a murder investigation.'

'I see, so you're treating me as a suspect in your investigation?'

Logan smiled, revealing his tobacco and coffee-stained teeth. 'Not at all, sir, but there are a number of points we wish to clear up regarding your dealings with the firm of Arkwright, Hislop and Pinder.'

'I've never seen or spoken to any of them. I was told by a secretary that they were playing golf in Portugal at the time I purchased my shares.'

'That is so, sir, but you did call upon Mr Roland Stratton, who was their company's general manager? We were told by his secretary that you had angry exchanges with Mr Stratton in his office.'

'Yes, I suppose I was angry when I saw him, particularly when he said that nothing could be done to recover any of the money I had entrusted to them, because the Linduana Copper Mining Company had crashed and its chief executive and others had absconded to Somalia with what money the company still held.'

'I can see you had every justification to be angry.'

'Yes, I certainly was angry. At the time I felt like giving that smarmy bastard Rackman a bloody good hiding!'

Logan's eyes widened and he looked steadily at Carson. 'Can you tell me where you were between 9 pm on Sunday, 12th October and 1 am the following morning?'

'I was here, watching television, reading, or in bed, trying to sleep.'

'Is there anyone who can verify your statement?'

'No, I now live alone. My wife died in August.'

'Logan's face softened. 'Oh, I'm very sorry to hear that, sir. She must have been quite young.'

'She was 51. She had a stroke and then a heart attack. Something else for your file on my personal history, Sergeant,' Carson said with deliberate sarcasm.

Logan looked slightly nonplussed before he replied. 'I just have one more question for you and then we'll go, sir. Can you tell me where you were last Saturday from late afternoon to the early hours of Sunday morning?'

'From about 5 pm I was travelling to Charing Cross. From 5.50 I was in the cocktail bar of the Charing Cross Hotel and for the rest of the evening I was in St. Martins Theatre watching "The Mousetrap," followed by an evening meal in an Italian restaurant, the name of which I have forgotten, but it was quite near the theatre. I got home by taxi some time after midnight. Now I have a question for you, Sergeant. What's this all about?'

'Because it was between these times that someone strangled Mr Roland Stratton in his car. Now, can anyone verify what you have said?'

'Yes, quite a number of people. A porter at Romford Railway Station, the barman in the cocktail bar at the Charing Cross Hotel, the woman at the theatre ticket office and an usherette in the theatre. Then there was the barman in the theatre cocktail lounge, the head waiter and the wine waiter in the Italian restaurant and the taxi driver who drove me home.' Carson decided not to mention Hurst. If he did he'd get a nuisance visit from the police and he didn't deserve that, after how generous he'd been.

'Have you got a recent photo of yourself, sir?'

'What do you want that for, your rogues gallery?' Carson said with a laugh.

'Not at all, it's simply to get verification from one of the people who you say saw you in London.'

Carson went to a sideboard, opened a top drawer and took out a photo album. Flicking through the pages, he selected a recent photo of himself in full uniform and handed it to Logan. 'Is there anything else, Sergeant?'

'No thank you, sir, but we may need to speak to you again some time.'

Carson led them to the front door and exchanged goodbyes with the two detectives.

\*\*\*

Back in their car and on their way to the police station, Logan turned to Holt, who was driving and said, 'What do you think about him - do you think he's our killer?'

'I can't be sure, but he seems quite a reasonable sort of guy, Sarge.'

Logan took Carson's photo out of his briefcase and studied it. 'This man was a sergeant major in the army, and sergeant majors are usually battle-hardened by the time they reach that rank. There can be little doubt that he has killed men during his service.'

'I see what you're getting at, Sarge, but killing an enemy in battle is a lot different to murdering someone in cold blood.'

'Well, I'd put money on it that he's our man,' Logan said as he put the photo back in his briefcase.

# CHAPTER SEVENTEEN

Detective Superintendent Braddock called a meeting in his office with DCI Warner, DI Ahmed and DS Logan.

'Update me on your progress with the Rackman and Stratton murders,' he began. 'I hope you've made some progress, because my ears are ringing with all the phone calls I've been getting from those in high places.'

'Well sir, we've all been working flat out on this case, but the number of people who bought shares from Rackman on behalf of the Linduana Copper Mining Company and need to be interviewed is tremendous,' Warner said.

'Yes, but the arrangement was that initially you only interview those who had made strong complaints to the stockbrokers or who had made very large investments. If this has been done, have any likely suspects been revealed?' Braddock replied.

'A number of very angry investors have been interviewed and a few were unable to account for their whereabouts at the times of the two murders. We are concentrating on this group and we'll probably see them again if no other likely suspects are forthcoming.'

'I interviewed a very likely suspect, sir,' Logan said excitedly.

Warner glared at Logan. Warner was one of the old school, who always knew his place and would never butt into a conversation between two senior officers.

'Who was that, Sergeant?' Braddock asked.

'It was an investor named Robert Carson, sir,' interposed Logan. 'We had a report from Stratton's secretary that Carson had had an angry exchange with Stratton. When questioned he said he was in a theatre in London at the time of Stratton's murder, but he was unable to name anyone who could verify his statement. When questioned regarding the death of Rackman he said he lived alone and was at home in bed at the time Rackman was killed.'

Braddock looked straight at Logan. 'Is that all you've got to go on to suggest that he's the killer?'

Logan looked uncomfortable. 'No, sir, but Carson is a former sergeant major in the army, an infantry soldier with battle experience. He was trained to kill and looks capable of doing so.'

'What a lot of twaddle, Sergeant! There's thousands of men in this country who've served in the army and been trained to kill, but thank God they don't carry on doing that when they leave the battlefields behind and come out of the army.' Braddock turned to Warner. 'If that's as far as you've got with this investigation, Owen, I'd like you to spread your net wider. I think DS Logan's hunch that Carson is the double killer is a pipe dream, but it might be worthwhile to have a word with his former commanding officer to get his opinion as to Carson's character.'

'Right, sir, I suggest DS Logan should accompany DI Ahmed for the interview,' Warner said, with a glance at Ahmed. Braddock nodded his agreement and pointed to his door. It was his way of telling his men that the meeting was over and it was time for them to get on with what they had to do.

# CHAPTER EIGHTEEN

Captain Justin Barker, the Adjutant of the 1ˢᵗ Battalion the Essex and Hertfordshire Light Infantry Regiment, tapped on his commanding officer's door and waited for Lieutenant Colonel Deacon's response.

'Enter!' Deacon almost shouted.

Barker entered and stood in front of Deacon's desk. 'The guard commander has brought two detectives to HQ, sir. They wish to see you. Shall I bring them in?'

'Any idea what it's all about, Justin?'

'They identified themselves as Detective Inspector Ahmed and Detective Sergeant Logan. They say they're investigating a very serious crime and wish to speak to you regarding former Sergeant Major Carson, sir.'

'All right, wheel them in, Justin.'

Barker left the office and returned a minute later with the two detectives. Deacon stood up. 'Sit yourselves down gentlemen, and tell me what you want to know about our former sergeant major. I can't believe he has broken any laws since he left the army.'

Ahmed and Logan sat down. Ahmed opened his briefcase and Logan took out his pocket book and ball-point.

'Sir, do you wish me to leave?' Barker said.

'No, please remain, Justin.'

Deacon sat down at his desk and clasped his hands across his chest. 'So, what do you want to know about Mr Carson that's not subject to the Official Secrets Act?'

'Well, to get straight to the point, Mr Carson invested in a copper mining company in Africa. He bought fifty thousand pounds worth of shares through the brokerage firm Arkwright, Hislop and Pinder. Unfortunately, the copper yield was well below what had been expected and the mining company crashed. To make matters worse for the investors, the CEO of the mining company and other senior officers of the company cleared the company's account and absconded to Somalia. As a result Mr Carson, along with many other investors, totally lost their investments...'

'I apologize for stopping you in full flow, but I still can't see why you should be taking such an interest in Carson. Are all the investors getting the same attention?'

Ahmed cleared his throat. 'As I was about to explain, sir many disgruntled investors threatened legal action against the brokerage company. Others, including Mr Carson, took a stronger line. It was reported to us by the secretary to Mr Stratton, the general manager, that Mr Carson and the general manager had a very heated exchange of words in his office.'

'From what you've said, it sounds to me as if Carson had every justification to have a go at the general manager.'

Ahmed sighed audibly. 'To continue, some time later the consultant who sold the shares to Carson was found dead in his home and Mr Stratton was found dead in his motorcar. Both men had been murdered. In the course of our investigation we interviewed Mr Carson and found that he was unable to provide a verifiable account of where he was at the time of these crimes.'

Deacon's eyes blazed. 'Are you suggesting that Mr Carson had something to do with the two murders? I can tell you without contradiction that he is a man of impeccable character. He is the holder of the Military Cross for bravery and has served his Queen and country and my regiment with distinction. He's no murderer. In battle he always showed mercy to wounded and surrendering enemy soldiers.'

'Are you suggesting that Carson is incapable of killing?'

'No, of course not. He was an infantry soldier who was trained to kill, and when he confronted an enemy in battle it was either he or the enemy soldier who had to die, or surrender. After nearly forty years of soldiering in war zones, he survived. Is there anything else you want to know about the best sergeant major I was ever privileged to command, Inspector?'

Ahmed looked red-faced. 'No sir, you've been very helpful.'

Ahmed stood up and Logan put his book and pen away and followed suit.

'Captain, please see that these detectives are escorted off the base,' Deacon said with a dismissive tone.

Barker led Ahmed and Logan out of the Deacon's office and detailed the orderly room chief clerk to escort the detectives to the guardroom.

***

Driving back to the police headquarters, Ahmed turned to Logan. 'Do you still think Carson is a double killer?'

'Yes, I do, guv. I wasn't taken in by that bloody Colonel Blimp type with all his praise for Carson. He was bound to defend him. The army is one of those outfits that always close their ranks when they're being opposed.'

'Blimey Paul, I never knew you were an authority on the British Army.'

'I'm not, but I have a younger brother who is a lieutenant in the Army Intelligence Corps and he tells me all about army traditions.'

'Anyway, getting back to Carson, you're going to need a lot more evidence of his guilt before the Super and the DCI are convinced. Not only that, you'll need to convince me before I support your case against Carson.'

'OK guv, I get your drift. I'll just keep digging until I get to the bottom of this case.'

Ahmed gave a short laugh. 'Just mind you don't fall down that hole you're digging.'

Logan sighed deeply and his hand tightened on the steering wheel. Neither spoke of the matter again during the drive back to the police station.

# CHAPTER NINETEEN

'There's a Mr Albert Arkwright at the desk, sir and he wants to see the Borough Commander, or whoever is investigating the death of Lance Rackman and Roland Stratton. I thought you'd want to deal with this one before it went to the Borough Commander,' the desk sergeant said.

'Put him in Interview Room 6, Sergeant, and tell him I'll be down to see him shortly,' replied DCI Warner.

Warner located the case file and buzzed through to DI Ahmed's office. 'We've got a visit from Albert Arkwright, the golf-playing stockbroker. Join me in Interview Room 6 straight away, Ahmed.'

Warner and Ahmed met at the top of the stairs and went down to the interview room on the ground floor. When they entered they found Arkwright sitting in the interviewee's chair, smoking a cheroot. He was deeply tanned, with thick grey hair, and his beady, almost black, eyes, gave him a shifty look.

'I'm DCI Warner and this is my colleague, DI Ahmed,

sir,' Warner said as he and Ahmed sat in the chairs on the other side of the table.

'I do hope you don't mind me smoking, gentlemen,' Arkwright said as he flicked ash from his cheroot on the floor.

'As you will have noticed, sir, there are no ashtrays provided, which is usually an indication that the room is a non-smoking zone. We do permit smoking in rooms where suspects are being interviewed and ashtrays are provided,' Warner said, with a slight smile.

'Well, as I'm not one of your suspects, I certainly wouldn't want to infringe any of your police regulations,' Arkwright said as he dropped the cheroot on the floor and crushed it with his shoe.

Warner winced slightly, but said nothing and opened a file. 'You must have had quite a shock when you heard the news of the death of two of your employees, sir.'

'Yes, I certainly did. It spoiled my holiday, so much so that I came home before I intended. Now that I'm here I should like you to advise me of the progress you have made in finding out who was responsible for the murder of two of my key employees.'

'We have made extensive enquiries and interviewed a large number of your clients, but because of the number of people involved in the enquiry we cannot narrow our search to deal with the most likely suspects in the case.'

Arkwright's raised eyebrows almost reached his hairline. 'From what you say, Chief Inspector, you believe that one of our clients was responsible for the murders.'

'Yes, it is my considered opinion that one or more of them was responsible. Our enquiries have established that many of your clients have made serious complaints and threats against your company over the matter of the Linduana Copper Mining Company's crash and the embezzlement of their investment funds by executives of that company.'

'Yes, that was a very unfortunate affair, but no blame can be attributed to my company,' Arkwright replied, with narrowed eyes.

'That's a matter of opinion, but the manner in which your business practices are conducted is not my concern. I am only concerned with investigating the murders of your two employees. Therefore, any information you can provide regarding the personal lives of the two victims might help with our enquiries. For example, it has been suggested that Lance Rackman was overly familiar with some of his female clients and sometimes exaggerated the high potential growth of the shares he was promoting.'

Arkwright's eyes widened and flashed. 'My partners and I had little day-to-day contact with any of our consultants. That was left to our general manager. On the odd occasions when we did talk to them, it was only about business matters. All I can say about Rackman is that he was the best investment consultant we ever employed and I'm sure we'll find it hard to replace a man of his calibre and work ethic.'

'So, you're telling me that you've never received any complaints from anyone about his personal behaviour or business practices, sir?'

Arkwright shook his head vigorously. 'Yes, Chief Inspector, I am, and I can also say that I've never had any complaints about any of my staff.'

Warner and Ahmed exchanged glances and Warner closed his file. 'Just one last question, sir can you tell me when you expect Mr Hislop and Mr Pinder to return from their golfing holiday?'

'I've no idea. I would have still been out there with them if it hadn't been for the news about the murders.'

'We'll need to talk to them. Can you arrange for them to be notified, or shall I get the Portuguese police to tell them?'

'No, don't involve the Portuguese police. I'll phone my partners this evening.'

'I hope you will stress to them that we need to speak to them as a matter of urgency.'

'Of course I shall. I'm very anxious that this matter is cleared up as soon as possible so I can arrange for the recruitment of replacement staff and get back to business. I shall, of course, expect you to keep me up to speed with your progress in solving this case.'

'We'll let you know when we make an arrest, sir. In the meantime, we may need to speak to you again. Goodbye, Mr Arkwright.' Arkwright muttered 'goodbye' as he stalked out of the room.

The two detectives went back to DCI Warner's office.

'Well, that was a waste of time, guv,' Ahmed said as he slumped into Warner's visitors' chair.

'Not entirely, Ahmed. We may not have gained anything worthwhile regarding the two murders, but Arkwright's manner and his apparent total lack of knowledge about his employees suggest to me that he and his two junior partners are just a trio of self-indulgent and money-grabbing wasters who are completely unfit to be running an investment brokerage. When Hislop and Pinders return from Portugal we'll give them a grilling, but I feel sure that they'll not provide anything more useful than we got from Arkwright.'

'Yes, I take your point, guv. It looks as though Rackman was operating how he liked and as long as he brought home the investments the partners gave him a free hand. Anyway, what do you want me to do now?'

'Just keep interviewing all the investors who don't have alibis for the times of the two murders, Ahmed. If we dig deep enough something has got to come to light.'

\*\*\*

Later that day Warner received a telephone call from Arkwright. 'Chief Inspector, I have just opened the company safe to find that a large sum of cash has been removed!' Arkwright said in a quavering voice.

'If you suspect that your safe has been burgled you should report it to your local police station. But, tell me, who had access to the safe and how much cash is missing?'

'My partners and the General Manager were the only people with keys to the safe.'

'Hmm. Then since you and your partners were away in Portugal, it would appear that the cash was removed by your general manager, or the person who killed him took his keys, got into your offices, opened the safe and stole the cash. If that is the case then the theft is linked to the murder of your Mr Stratton, which puts it on my plate. I'll send a detective and a forensic team to check the safe. Will you be there?'

'Yes, I'm acting as general manager and my secretary, Ms Tate, will be in attendance.'

'That's good, because she'll need to be seen. Something else - leave the safe exactly as you found it.'

'I hope your people won't be too long, I have an engagement tonight.'

'Okay, then I'll send the team tomorrow morning. Please make sure you're there then.'

'I'll make every effort to be there by 9 am,' Arkwright replied and put down the phone.

\*\*\*

'So, what's the score on the missing cash from Arkwright's safe, Ahmed?'

'The SOCO boys couldn't find any trace of a break-in or foreign fingerprints on the safe and apart from the £120,000 which Arkwright claimed was in the safe, nothing else was missing, guv.'

'What was Arkwright's explanation for the money in the safe?'

'He said it related to an investment by a Russian businessman who was visiting the country with the intention of settling here,' Paul said with a wide grin.

Warner smiled knowingly. 'I get the distinct impression that you doubt that there was that much cash in the safe, Ahmed.'

'Well it does seem to be a lot of petty cash to be held in a small office. If it was payments for shares, which are usually made by cheque or bank transfer, it would normally be paid into a bank account. I can't see any reason for that not to have been done unless, of course, it was a case of money-laundering.'

'So you think there was no burglary and that it might be some sort of insurance scam?'

'No, I think that's most unlikely. I believe Stratton's killer took his keys, let himself into the building, opened the safe, took the money out, relocked the safe and took the keys back to Stratton's car and placed the keys in Stratton's pocket.'

'Good for you, Ahmed! That's some theory. It would make a lot of sense if the killer was one of the investors, someone who had lost a considerable amount of money. His warped mind would make him think he had every justification for taking the cash. The only snag is that the keys were found in Stratton's pocket.'

'Yes, but the killer could have put them back there after he had left the building and was returning to his own car, which he had probably parked near Stratton's,' Ahmed replied.

'If that's what happened, it suggests we're dealing with a very cool-headed individual. Get your section to re-interview all the investors who invested more than £40,000 in that crooked copper company.'

# CHAPTER TWENTY

It was early evening; Carson had eaten his supper, as he chose to call it. He washed the used crockery and pots, put them away and settled in his favourite armchair with a black coffee and brandy on his side table. He picked up the mystery paperback he had bought a few weeks before. So far he had found little time to make any headway with the complexities of the story.

The doorbell disturbed his concentration. He sighed deeply, put the novel down and went to the front door. He switched on the passage light and opened the front door to see Hurst, wearing a brown trilby and an army officer's raincoat, both which were soaking wet.

Before Carson could say anything, Hurst stepped into the passage. 'I'm sorry if I'm disturbing you, Bob, but not having heard from you for some time, I thought I'd pop over to see how you were.'

'No, you're not disturbing anything of importance, but it

would have been better if you had given me a call before you came. Anyway get those wet togs off and join me for a warming drink.'

'Yes, I'm sorry about that. It was rather remiss of me. I'll remember to do that next time I visit you.' He removed his hat and coat and hung them on the hallstand.

'How did you get so wet, Roger?' Carson said, as he led Hurst into the sitting room.

'It's raining cats and dogs and I couldn't find anywhere nearby to park.'

Carson went to a sideboard and took out a bottled of malt whisky and a glass. 'I hope you're still on the whisky, Roger,' he said as he poured a double measure into the glass and handed it to Hurst.

'That's the spirit, Bob,' he replied as he took a deep swig from the glass and made himself comfortable on the sofa.

'Well, as you can see, Roger, I'm pretty well established here and as fit and healthy as I can expect for a man of my years. Does that satisfy your wish to know how I am?'

'Yes, you really do look fit for your age. I'm 44 and you must be at least ten years older than me.'

'I'm 56 next birthday. But can we get down to the real reason for your visit?'

Hurst ran his fingers through his thinning brown hair before he answered. 'I don't like to bring up the subject of your investment with that dodgy African copper company, but I wondered if you had seen the news about the murder of the general manager of the brokerage firm you dealt with?'

'Oh, that case. Yes, I did catch the item on television news. Some psychopathic investor must have been sorely aggrieved with the firm to have killed its general manager. Roland Stratton was his name. Actually I had angry words with him, which didn't get me any of my money back. I went to the Financial Ombudsman, but I was told there was no case for any action to be taken against Messrs Arkwright, Hislop and Pinder, the firm's senior partners.'

Hurst leaned forward and looked straight at Carson. 'But you did have quite a strong motive for revenge,' he almost whispered. 'Would it be out order for me to suggest that you did away with both the firm's ace consultant and its general manager?'

'Yes, it bloody well would!' Carson snapped back. 'You must be out of your mind to think I'd murder two people because I'd been taken in by a smart-arse salesman! For your information, I have resolved to put it all behind me and see if I can get some sort of work to help pay for me to emigrate to Australia.'

Hodge's face reddened. 'I really am sorry to have misjudged you. I just thought you had every justification to take some sort of revenge against the brokerage firm.'

'No, not me, but it seems likely that some investor has done so. But let's change the subject.'

Hurst gave a humourless laugh. 'I agree. So, what kind of a job do you have in mind?'

'I haven't given it much thought up to now. I might try to get some sort of security work.'

Hurst looked thoughtful and rubbed the greying stubble on his chin. 'There's not much available in that line of work at the moment. You might be able to get a job as a department store floor walker, a traffic warden, a bailiff or a bodyguard.'

'Huh! I can't see myself doing those sorts of jobs, but like you I haven't any experience, other than nearly forty years of being an infantry soldier.'

'Yes, and a damned good soldier, as everybody from the Colonel down to the most junior private in the battalion would agree.'

Carson smiled. 'So you've forgiven me for my part in the prosecution at your court martial?'

'Nothing's truer than that, Sergeant Major. I had plenty of time in detention and afterwards to mull over the case. I remembered how you saved our arses, twice. I'll always recall the time when my platoon was in danger of being overrun and probably wiped out when you led a couple of rifle teams from Charlie Company to repel and finally beat off the outnumbering attacking force. That's when you got your gong, wasn't it? And very well deserved.'

'Yes, the Military Cross, which doesn't count for very much when you're back in Civvy Street. Anyway, what's all this about? You'll be giving me a swollen head. You were no slouch when it came to taking on anything that came your way and if it hadn't been for you going over the top with that prisoner, you'd have soon moved up through the ranks. It's rather sad, but we can't change history, so let's back to talking about my job prospects.'

'Yes, and I think I might have the answer. My firm is always looking for replacement debt collectors. A lot of our new boys are too weak in their approach, or they go overboard and make all sorts of silly threats against the debtors and then don't complete their probationary period. With your commanding presence and no-nonsense sergeant major-approach you'd have no trouble in bringing the bacon home. The pay isn't very good but you do get five percent of everything you manage to collect. Would you like me to introduce you to my manager?'

'Thanks for the offer, Roger. I'll need to give it some thought,'

'Good. When you've made up your mind, give me a ring and I'll arrange a meeting for you. Now, if you can spare another whisky before I leave, I shall be most grateful.'

'Yes, it might be the right time for you to leave. I see it's stopped raining, but it's forecast to return before morning.'

# CHAPTER TWENTY-ONE

'We're here to see Detective Chief Inspector Warner, Sergeant,' said the taller of the two men. Both were late middle-aged, expensively suited and sun-tanned.

'What are your names, sir?'

'I'm Desmond Hislop and this gentleman is George Pinder. We are stockbrokers and we're here at the request of the Detective Chief Inspector. He wants to talk to us about the murder of two of our employees.'

'Oh, I see, I'll get on to the DCI straight away,' the sergeant said. He walked to the rear of the enquiry desk to telephone DCI Warner. 'I've got two gents by the names of Hislop and Pinder in reception, sir.'

'Get them brought up to my office, Sergeant.'

The sergeant turned to a constable who was sitting at the back of the office inputting the details of found property items into a computer.

'PC Nicholls, take these two gentlemen up to the DCI's office.'

Nicholls came around to the front of the reception desk and led the two men to a flight of stairs. 'The DCI's office is on the first floor, so it's not worth taking the lift,' he told them.

The two men laughed. 'Climbing stairs is one way of keeping fit, Constable,' said Hislop. 'We do it by playing three or four games of golf every week.'

Nicholls half-smiled but did not reply. 'This is the DCI's office' he said, tapping on a door marked "DCI Owen Warner".

'Come in!' Warner shouted.

Nicholls and the two men entered the office and stood in the centre of the room. Warner rose from his chair. 'Please sit down gentlemen,' he said, pointing to two easy chairs in front of his desk. 'Nicholls, return to reception. I'll give you a buzz when I want you to escort these two gentlemen out of the building.'

'I'm DCI Warner and this is DI Ahmed,' he said, pointing to Ahmed, who was sitting at the side of his desk.

Hislop leaned forward in his chair. 'I do hope getting us back at short notice from our golfing holiday won't be a waste of time for either of us,' he said.

'So do I, sir. Shall we begin by you telling us all you can about the money that was stolen from the safe in your general manager's office?'

Hislop and Pinder, clearly alarmed, turned and looked at each other. 'What money?' they said in unison to Warner.

'I refer to the £120,000 that your Mr Arkwright reported stolen from the safe. Are you both telling me that neither of you had any knowledge of its existence?'

'I can say, with the utmost certainty, that I have no knowledge of such an amount of cash being held in the safe,' Hislop said.

'That goes for me as well' Pinder blurted out. 'We never held such an amount in cash. The majority of payments for shares are made by cheque or bank transfers. On the rare occasions that payments are made by cash they were promptly banked as soon as they are received.'

'Are you suggesting that Mr Arkwright is lying about the money?' Ahmed interposed.

'Good heavens, no!' Hislop replied. 'There must be some other explanation. Perhaps it was his own money he had put in the safe. He's had several attempted burglaries on his home and might have thought the money would be more secure in our safe. It's virtually burglar-proof. The only people who had access were Mr Arkwright and us.'

'I really can't see what all your questions about the contents of our safe have to do with your investigation into the murder of our two employees,' Pinder angrily snapped.

Warner leaned forward and glared at Pinder. 'For your information, there is a strong possibility that the money was stolen from your safe, which wasn't in any way damaged, but opened with the only key available to the thief - Roland Stratton's. I am assuming, of course, that the keys held by you and your partners would not be left where they could be found when you were away playing golf. From our investigations it has become strongly evident that the killer took Stratton's keys after he killed him. This enabled him to gain access to your offices, open the safe in your general manager's office and remove the money. The only question that has to be answered is, did the killer know that the safe contained such a large amount of cash, or was he simply looking for something detrimental about your company's business practices, and came upon the cash by chance?'

'That's absolute nonsense!' Hislop snapped. 'Our business practices are completely honourable and transparent. And furthermore, none of your preposterous theories have anything to do with us. We were both away in Portugal when the murders and burglary occurred. We know nothing about the personal lives of Roland Stratton and Lance Rackman. All we can say about them is that they were both efficient and loyal employees.'

Warner closed his case file and turned to Ahmed. 'Is there anything you want to add, DI Ahmed?'

Ahmed shook his head. 'No, sir, I've heard enough.'

Warner picked up his phone and rang the desk sergeant. 'Send PC Nicholls up here to escort our visitors out of the building.'

As soon as Nicholls arrived, Warner addressed Hislop and Pinder. 'Thank you for attending this interview, gentlemen. I do hope it will not be necessary to see you again. Goodbye.'

After they had left, Warner sat back in his chair and rubbed his eyes. 'Ahmed, this job gets worse every day. Thank heavens I'm retiring next year.'

Ahmed gave a short laugh. 'Yes, it sure as hell does, especially when you have to deal with the Hislops and Pinders of life.'

'I suppose we'd better let the Super hear what we've learned from those two golfing fruitcakes, Ahmed.'

'Yeah, but it wasn't very much help to our investigation, guv.'

Warner picked up his phone and dialled the Detective Superintendent's number. Braddock answered immediately.

'Ahmed and I have interviewed Arkwright's partners, Hislop and Pinder, sir. I'm afraid it was a case of wasting police time. Both claimed they had no knowledge of the money, but suggested that it might have belonged to Arkwright. It smells of money-laundering to me, sir.'

'And to me, Owen,' Braddock replied. 'Don't waste any more time on the money. When we finally apprehend the killer, we'll look in to the matter of the money. In the meantime give priority to reviewing what you've learnt about the investors who were the biggest losers.'

'Right, boss I'll get on to it and keep you informed of any progress.'

'You heard all that, Ahmed, so get your team to dig deeper into the backgrounds of the major investors. One of them has to be the killer.'

# CHAPTER TWENTY-TWO

Albert Arkwright was chairing a meeting in his office with Desmond Hislop and George Pinder.

'The police haven't said any more about the money that was taken from our safe. They probably imagine it was our late general manager who had put it there, for reasons best known only by him. That being the case they won't come sniffing around to unearth our little money-laundering ploy.'

'Yes, that's all right Albert, but you were the one that reported the theft to them,' said Hislop.

'I know, but I never gave them any information about why it was there,' Arkwright retorted.

'But don't forget that those two detectives who interviewed George and me asked what we knew about it,' said Pinder. 'We suggested that you might have put it in the safe because you had had a couple of attempted burglaries at your home.'

'That's okay then, because if they come back to me on it,

I can tell them it must have been a private arrangement by Stratton, which I wasn't aware of, but gave him permission to keep it in the safe temporarily. With him now out of the picture that's the last we'll hear about it. That is of course, unless they catch Stratton's killer and recover some or all of the money. It'll still be a loss to us because the money will have to go to his widow. But I didn't call you in to dwell on that matter. I've been busy hiring replacement staff. I want to introduce them to you.'

Both Hislop and Pinder looked pointedly at Arkwright. 'Don't you think it would have been more correct to invite us to attend the interviews?' Hislop said.

Arkwright half laughed. 'Of course, old chap, but the replacements were urgently needed and you both wanted to get back to Portugal in a hurry. Anyway, they are all assembled in Sharon's office. I'll give her a buzz and she'll bring them up here for your inspection. The new general manager is Keith Dawlish. He's never been up to the same standard as Stratton or Rackman, but he's a loyal and hardworking consultant and I thought it better to appoint someone we knew rather than take a chance on an unknown outsider. I didn't want Dawlish to come this afternoon. You both know him well enough and I didn't want the newcomers to know that he was new to the job.'

Hislop and Pinder nodded agreement.

Arkwright buzzed Sharon on the intercom. She answered immediately.

'You can bring them up now, Sharon,' he told her.

Two minutes elapsed before Sharon entered Arkwright's office, followed by three smartly-dressed men. They were all in their thirties and alert looking. They stood in the centre of the office waiting for permission to sit in the three chairs set out in front of Arkwright's desk.

'Please be seated, gentlemen,' Arkwright said, pointing to the chairs. 'You may leave us, Sharon.'

After Sharon left, Arkwright introduced Hislop and Pinder to the three men. Then, to Hislop and Pinder, he said, 'These are our new client consultants'. He pointed from left to right in turn. 'Barry Drummond, Jason Prior and Stuart Carter. They've all had at least five years' experience in the stockbrokerage business.' He turned to Hislop and Pinder. 'Have you any questions you'd like to ask them?'

Hislop and Pinder shook their heads in unison. 'No, Albert, I'm sure George will agree with me that you will have asked all the questions necessary when you interviewed these gentlemen,' said Hislop. Pinder nodded his agreement.

'Splendid! Then all I need to say is welcome aboard, Barry, Jason and Stuart,' Arkwright said with a quick smile. 'Sharon will now take you down to meet Keith Dawlish, our general manager. No doubt he will no doubt have much to say to you about what is expected of you in carrying out your consultative role with our large client base of investors.'

Arkwright buzzed for Sharon. She arrived within a minute and led the three men down to the general manager's office. As soon as the door closed Hislop said, 'There's just one question I'd like answered, Albert.'

'And what's that, Desmond?' Arkwright snapped testily.

'Why did you employ three new consultants?'

'To put it simply, we have promoted Dawlish and replaced Rackman with two. We could never expect to get the same work effort from one man we had from Rackman.'

'I take your point, but we don't need to pay the replacements as much as Rackman and Dawlish.'

'Of course not, we'll just see how they progress and adjust their salaries and bonuses accordingly.'

'That sounds okay by me,' Pinder added.

'Right, that's enough chat about the new staff, because there's something else I want to talk about. I've been thinking about hiring a private detective to see if he can do any better than the police have done so far. I don't see that any of our regular investors would go to the lengths of killing our staff over the failure of their shares to increase in value. I'm of the view that whoever was responsible is someone who couldn't afford to lose his investment. Sharon has produced a list of all our clients who invested in the Linduana Copper Mining Company. She has highlighted the first-time investors. There were only about ten, and one of those is a man named Robert Carson, who had angry words with Stratton and threatened to take further action against our company. Sharon said Rackman had told her that Carson was a retired soldier who was planning to emigrate to Australia and hoped that his investment would grow, to enable him to settle in a new home there. You need to be young and have technical skills or a lot of money to settle in Australia. Carson was in his fifties, without any useful skills. He's lost most of the money he had and being naïve about the way shares can rise and fall in value he blames our company for his loss. A loss that was worsened by Linduana's CEO and his cronies absconding with what money remained of the investments we made on behalf of our clients. To my mind Carson is a man who might be strongly motivated enough to take revenge on those he feels have thwarted his plans. If you agree, I'll get Sharon to check out a reliable detective agency, with a view to hiring someone.'

'I agree with that, as long as it doesn't cost us too much,' said Hislop.

'I've got just the man to do the job for us,' Pinder said excitedly. 'He's the husband of a cousin of mine. His name is Bruce Hardwick. He's a retired detective chief inspector who has set himself up as a private investigator. He works alone and is not connected in any way with an agency.'

Arkwright stroked his chin in thought. 'Hmm, he sounds right for what I have in mind. But I'd like to keep this arrangement in house. I don't want the police to get to know what we're doing. Get in touch with him George, and ask him if he'd be prepared to carry out some work for us. Don't give him any more details than that. I'll tell him all he needs to know when I see him. If he's agreeable to work for us, get him to contact me direct to arrange an appointment. I don't have anything else to say and if you two haven't either, let's get back to our long-suffering golf widow wives.'

# CHAPTER TWENTY-THREE

'Mr Hardwick is here, sir. Shall I bring him up?'

'Yes please, Sharon,' Arkwright replied. Sharon ushered Hardwick into Arkwright's office.

'Please take a seat Mr Hardwick,' Arkwright said, pointing to an easy chair in front of his desk.

'Shall I stay?' Sharon said.

'No, that won't be necessary. I'll give you a buzz if I need you.'

'Good afternoon, Mr Hardwick.'

'Bruce will be fine, sir,' Hardwick said.

Arkwright gave him a quick once-over. Hardwick was a sallow-faced, sharp-eyed, thick-set, middle-aged man who looked every inch a policeman.

'Before I explain what we'd like you to investigate for us, I'd like you to give me a brief summary of your police experience,' Arkwright began.

Hardwick gave a quick frown. He wasn't used to his clients questioning his background. 'I served for thirty years in the Metropolitan Police. Most of my time was as a detective in the ranks of detective constable to detective chief inspector.'

'Did you investigate many homicides?'

'Yes, I certainly did and, I might add, very successfully.'

'That's good, because I want you to investigate a case of double murder. Would you be prepared to deal with that?'

Hardwick looked steadily at Arkwright before he replied. 'Investigating murders is not usually undertaken by private enquiry agents in this country. The police certainly discourage such practice. I take it the case is being investigated by the police?'

'Yes, but not very successfully, I'm afraid.'

'Ah, you must be referring to the murder of two of your employees. I recall reading about it in the press and seeing interviews about it on television. As I understand it a man called Rackman was murdered in his home by a suspected burglar. Then a man named Stratton was strangled in his car.'

'Yes, I see you are aware of the basic details, Bruce.'

'I'll have to be honest with you, I can't see that I could do any better than the police. They have access to all the forensic evidence gathered and they must have interviewed all the known suspects in the case.'

'The known suspects you mention are investors who are represented by my company. Briefly, the Linduana Copper Mining Company, to which we were investing, on their behalf, crashed and our clients lost their investments.'

'Good grief! You surely can't expect me to go over all that the police have already done. That could take me months. To be frank I'd not be prepared to spend such time when I have plenty of work on divorce cases, tracing missing persons, background checks and the like to keep me busy.'

'No, I don't expect you to do that. I'm ninety-nine per cent certain that we know who did it, and with the right sort of interrogation and checking of his alibis, you could crack the case for us. If you did you'd be would be well rewarded and your success would be a feather in your cap, I'm sure. Aside from that, we're very keen for our clients to be reassured that we are a company anxious to restore our credibility and strength of purpose when we are confronted with serious problems. So, how do you feel now about taking on the job?'

Hardwick took a deep breath and licked his lips. 'Yes, in those circumstances I'll do what I can do to find the killer. I should warn you though, my fees are considered to be high by some of my clients and I do require all my likely expenses to be paid up front.'

Arkwright nodded and smiled. 'I'm sure we can come to a mutually satisfactory arrangement. Please submit your accounts to Sharon Tate, for the attention of our general manager, Keith Dawlish. As to your investigations, I should like you to submit a daily report to me personally. For this purpose an email will suffice. This is my address.' He handed a card to Hardwick. Hardwick glanced at it and slipped it into the top pocket of his jacket.

'Will that be all then, Mr Arkwright?'

'Yes, I'm sure you can find your way down to Sharon's office. She has a file for you. It has all the details we have about the case. It includes the name and address of our number one suspect. I look forward to receiving your progress reports. Au revoir, Bruce.'

'Cheerio for now, Albert,' Hardwick said with a short laugh as he walked out of the office.

# CHAPTER TWENTY-FOUR

Detective Sergeant Paul Logan had been detailed by DI Ahmed to check all pawnbrokers and jewellers in the area, to see if Lance Rackman's gold Rolex watch or diamond ring had been proffered to them for pawning or sale. He had spent most of his shift in his search and there was only one pawnshop left on his list. He knew the owner, a shifty character. Logan was wise to his sometimes dubious business practices - dubious to the point of lawbreaking - but he had a reputation for always being helpful to the police.

Logan entered the shop to see its owner perched on a high stool examining a brooch through a magnifying glass.

'Hello, Kovac.'

The man slid awkwardly off the stool and leaned on the counter. 'Good afternoon, Mr Logan. How can I be of help to you?' he said in an obsequious tone.

Logan studied Kovac's wrinkled and raddled face. This old bugger was on his way out.

'Have you had anyone in here trying to flog or pawn a Rolex gold wristwatch or a man's diamond ring?'

Kovac squinted at Logan and ran a heavily blue-veined hand through his fluffy white hair. 'Rolex watches? I don't see many of those these days. Especially gold ones,' he said, opening his mouth to reveal his almost toothless jaw. 'If I'd had one through my hands I wouldn't forget that. But I've had a few young fellas in here with diamond rings to pawn, or sell. Mostly returned engagement rings, I'd say.'

'This is important to me. You do keep records of the stuff you take in pawn or buy, don't you?'

'Yes, of course I do, I record every transaction.' He rummaged under the counter and produced a dog-eared A4-sized book. He opened it and ran his finger down a list of entries. 'Yeah, here's one I got a couple of weeks ago. The bloke wanted to sell it. It must have been worth a couple of grand, but I got him to accept a hundred quid.'

'What was his name?' Logan almost shouted.

'Here, look for yourself,' Kovac said, spinning the book around and pointing to the entry.

The writing was almost illegible, but Logan could just decipher the name and address of the seller: Robert Carson, 52 Glendale Road, Romford.

'Gotcha!' he almost shouted.

'Is he the bloke you're after, Mr Logan?'

Logan smiled smugly, 'He sure as hell is. The ring now becomes evidence in a criminal case, so let me have it and I'll give you an official receipt.'

Kovac frowned and said something in a foreign tongue. 'Are you sure I'll get it back?'

Logan gave a little laugh. 'Come on, hand it over. You know the rules about stolen property, Kovac.'

Kovac shuffled away to the rear of the shop, opened a drawer and took out a ring box with a label attached. He placed the box on the counter. Logan opened it and took out the ring. He took a pad of receipts from his pocket and made out one with the details contained on the label attached to the box. Then he tore out the top copy of the receipt and handed it to Kovac. He then copied the name and address of the seller into his pocket book.

'Now I don't want you to go blabbing about this case to any of your cronies or anyone else who comes in to enquire about the man who sold you the ring. Understand?'

'Yes, Mr Logan, you can trust me. I shan't talk about this matter to anyone else.'

'That's what I wanted to hear, Kovac,' Logan said. He laid a ten-pound note on the counter and walked out of the shop without a word.

'Thank you, Mr Logan and goodbye,' Kovac called after him.

*\*\*\**

The following morning DS Logan could not wait to contact DI Ahmed to give him the news of his success in obtaining Lance Rackman's diamond ring. Both he and Ahmed were attending the morning briefing, which was being conducted by DCI Warner. When the briefing was over Logan followed Ahmed to his office.

'I've got some great news for you, guv. I've got hold of Lance Rackman's diamond ring,' Logan said. He pulled a plastic property bag from his jacket pocket, took the ring out and showed it to Ahmed.

'Yes, that's a diamond ring, Paul, but how do you know it's Rackman's?'

'Because it was sold to a pawnbroker by Robert Carson,' Logan replied with a smug smile.

'If what you say is accurate that is certainly something to follow up on. We'll take your news to the DCI. He'll be delighted to hear of your success. I've got the case file in my pending tray. I'll take it to him and you can make a verbal report of the matter.'

Ahmed led the beaming Logan to DCI Warner's office.

'Good morning, boss. DS Logan has some news that might make your day,' Ahmed said and placed the case file on Warner's desk.

'Good, sit down and tell me what you you've got, Sergeant.'

Logan took out his pocket book and gave a rambling account of his visits to a score or more jewellers and pawnbrokers. 'The last one I visited, owned by a man named Kovac, is where Rackman's ring was sold for £100 by Robert Carson, the major suspect in the double murder case we are investigating.'

'Has the ring been identified as the one that was removed from the body of Rackman, Sergeant?'

'Well, no, sir, but it must be, because it was sold by Carson the suspect.'

'What proof have you that Carson sold the ring?'

'Carson gave his name and address to Kovac.'

'Oh, how very convenient that was for you, Sergeant! But surely it is hardly likely if the man was a murderer and the ring was a clue to his guilt. Wouldn't you think he would have used any name but his own?'

'Well, he did give his address as well, sir,'

'Which was?'

Logan opened his pocket book and read out the address he had entered, 52 Glendale Road, Romford. Warner opened the case file and read out the address that had been recorded when Carson had first been interviewed. It was 20 Phoenix Road, Romford.

'Yes, I suppose that's odd that he used his own name, but a different address. I'm sorry I forgot Carson's address, sir,' Logan said in a sheepish voice.

'There's something else that's very odd, Sergeant. Don't you think it rather strange that the man who sold the ring accepted £100 for it without question, when it must have been obvious that it was worth much more? Only an idiot would have taken the risk of being identified for such a paltry amount.'

'Yes, I suppose that is, strange, sir.'

'To me, this all smacks of a frame-up by the real killer. What you've got to do now is to find someone who can identify the ring as Rackman's - his colleagues or his housekeeper might be able to do that. Next you need to have Carson on an identification parade and get Kovac to attend to see if he can identify him as the man who sold him the ring. Of course, you must now realize that all this should have been done before you presented your report. You are a detective sergeant and I expect a more thorough job from those of that rank. So, if you wish to remain in your present rank, let alone aspire to a higher one, you should in future not jump to unfounded conclusions without a careful analysis of the factual evidence in the case you are investigating. That is all. Return to your duties, Sergeant!'

As soon as Logan had left the office, Warner gave a long sigh. 'Things are not what they used to be. Logan needs closer supervision. See that he gets it, Ahmed.'

'I'll see to that, boss. Unfortunately, he does sometimes give me the impression that he resents me being his superior officer.'

'You're not suggesting that he has racist tendencies, are you?'

'No, I think he considers himself superior to me because he is longer in service and five years older.'

'He might have some justification to think that if he'd passed the inspectors' promotion examination, rather than think he's worthy of advancement simply because of his age and experience.'

'Yes, I have to agree with your opinion. However, I have to say that in spite of his error of judgement in this case, he does try hard, and when he thinks he's on to something he's like a bull terrier and won't let go!'

'Then put him on a shorter lead, Ahmed,' Warner said with a laugh.

# CHAPTER TWENTY-FIVE

When DS Logan took the diamond ring to show to Lance Rackman's former housekeeper, Mrs Martha Pomeroy, he did not have to introduce himself. She recognized him as one of the detectives who had first entered Rackman's bungalow.

'Oh, hallo, Sergeant, what brings you back? I thought you'd all finished questioning me.'

'Well, almost Martha, I just have something to show you. May I come in? I won't keep you long.'

'Yes, of course, and you're just in time for a cup of tea. I was making one for my elevenses when you knocked on the door.'

Logan followed her into her neat and very tidy sitting room. A tray bearing tea-making materials and a plate of chocolate digestive biscuits was on the sofa table.

'Please take a seat and I'll pour the tea. You do take sugar, don't you?'

'Yes I do, but I don't want to put you to any trouble. I'd

like you to have a look at a piece of jewellery that I'm hoping you will recognize.'

Logan removed the ring from the property bag and held it out to her in his palm. 'Have you seen this ring before?'

'Yes, I do. I saw enough of it when I was working for Mr Rackman. I recognize that very large diamond which gives off such a bright sparkle.'

'Would you be prepared to make a statement that it is the same ring?'

'Yes, if that's all there's to it.'

Logan produced a statement form from his inside jacket pocket. 'I'll write it up, as you said, and you will just have to sign it,' he said with a warm smile.

Logan quickly wrote the statement and read it out to her. 'Do you agree with what I've written?' he said when he had finished.

'Oh, yes, I'm sure it's Mr Rackman's ring.'

'Then please sign immediately below the last line I have written,' he said and handed her the statement and his pen.

Martha signed the form and returned it to Logan, who folded it neatly and returned it to his jacket pocket.

'I'm now ready for a cup of tea and one of your chocolate digestives,' Logan said with a smug smile. He was delighted at getting the proof of ownership of the ring. He would show them all. All he needed was for Carson to be identified by Kovac and he'd cracked it.

On returning to the police station Logan showed his statement to DI Ahmed.

'That's good, Paul,' his boss replied.

'Thanks, guv, I'll be here with bells on to see Kovac identify Carson.'

Ahmed winced visibly. 'Don't set your hopes too high for

solving the case, Paul. Don't count your chickens until they are hatched.'

Logan was waiting in the reception area when a constable arrived with Kovac. The constable ushered Kovac into an interview room. 'Please wait here until you are required to view the identification parade,' he told him.

'Hello, Kovac, I'm glad you're here,' Logan said as he entered the room. 'When I came to your shop I should have asked you for a description of the man who sold you the ring. Did he have any major distinguishing features?'

'I can't remember much about how he looked. But I recall that he had a large beard and moustache and wore heavily-framed glasses.'

'How was he dressed?'

Kovac scratched his chin in thought. 'I think he was wearing a cap and a scarf.'

'How tall was...'

Logan was cut short by the entrance of Ahmed. 'Stay here Logan. I'll take Mr Kovac to
the viewing room.'

Ahmed led Kovac to a room next to where the identification parade was assembled, under the charge of the duty inspector.

'You will be able to see the line-up through this window, but no one in that room will be able to see you. The men will be numbered from one to eight from the left. Study each man, and if you recognize the man who sold you the ring, tell me his number. Is all that clear for you?'

'Yes, I understand, Inspector.'

Kovac peered through the one-way mirror. His eyes moving back and forth along the line of men for about five minutes.

'Do you recognize anyone?' Ahmed said.

Kovac turned and shook his head. 'I've never clapped eyes on any of those blokes before.'

'Well thank you for attending Mr Kovac, and I'm sorry it was all rather a waste of time.' 'That's okay, Inspector. But can you tell me when I'll get the ring back?'

'I'm afraid that as the ring is stolen property and should not have been sold, it will probably be passed to Mr Rackman's next-of-kin. In any event it will remain with us as evidence until the case is finalized.'

'So I'll be a hundred quid out of pocket on this one, Inspector.'

'Yes, I'm afraid so. Perhaps next time you are offered an item of value in such circumstances you will thoroughly check the identity and address of the seller. Goodbye Mr Kovac.'

'Cheerio,' muttered Kovac as he shuffled out of the building.

Ahmed joined the duty inspector and the members of the identification parade, who were waiting to be paid for their attendance. He took Carson aside. 'Please come with me, sir,' he said and led him into an interview room.

'Am I free to leave now, Inspector?' Carson asked in an unruffled tone.

'Yes of course, and I must apologize for the manner in which you have been called to prove your innocence. You may now take it that you are no longer considered a suspect in the case under investigation.'

'Thank you for that, Inspector, and goodnight,' Carson said as he walked out of the police station.

# CHAPTER TWENTY-SIX

Detective Superintendent Ralph Braddock was at home with his wife watching an early evening broadcast of the news when the doorbell rang.

'Who can be calling at this time of the day?' said his wife. 'Are you expecting anyone, Ralph?'

Braddock rose from his chair. 'No dear, but I'll answer the door rather than let it remain a mystery.'

Braddock opened the front door and was surprised to see the caller was ex-Detective Chief Inspector Bruce Hardwick, his former superior officer.

'You're the last person I'd expect to call,' said Braddock. 'But I'm pleased to see you after so long.'

'I hope I haven't called at a bad time, Ralph.'

'No, not at all, old chap. Jill and I were just watching the news. Come in and tell me what you've been up to these last nine or ten years, since you left the force.'

Hardwick took off his raincoat and hung it on the

hallstand. He followed Braddock into the sitting room.

'Look who's here, my old boss, Bruce Hardwick. You remember him don't you, Jill?'

'I certainly do. How could one forget the best dance partner in the police club?'

Hardwick gave Jill a quick hug. 'You've not changed much, Jill. You still look like the Belle of the Ball.'

'Yes, and you're still the same old flatterer,' Jill said with a laugh. 'Now I expect you two old pals would like to be left alone for a while to talk over your past times together. So I'll disappear into the bedroom to watch the rest of the news, which is followed by Morse, my favourite fictional detective. Do you want me to make you any coffee before I leave you, Ralph?'

'No love, we'll make do with Scotch.'

'Try not to overdo it, you know our doctor keeps warning you about the danger of drinking too much.'

'Yes, I know Jill, that's what doctors say to all their patients. Now, off you go to enjoy Chief Inspector Morse – he's a real boozer.'

Jill gave a little laugh and left the room. Braddock turned off the television, went to a cupboard and lowered the flap-style door to reveal a row of bottles and shelves containing glasses and decanters in a variety of shapes.

'What's your poison these days, still whisky and water, Bruce?'

'You can forget the water and add another measure of Scotch, Ralph,' Hardwick said with a laugh.

Braddock poured two doubles and set the glasses down on the sofa table, then sat next to Hardwick on the sofa. They both took swigs of their drinks before either spoke.

'Belated congratulations on your promotion to superintendent,' said Hardwick. 'I always knew you'd make it to superintendent or higher.'

'I don't expect to make it any higher, Bruce. Things are not the same as they used to be. There's too much interference from all those at the top. But how did you know I'd been promoted?'

Hardwick tapped his nose. 'Oh, I just keep my eyes and ears open. I don't miss very much of what goes on in the police service.'

'Hmm, you must be pushing sixty now. Have you retired, or landed a cushy job as a chief security officer for one of the large retail outlets?'

'No, nothing like that, I'm now what is sometime described as a gumshoe.'

'You mean a private investigator?'

'Yes, that's it. I work alone, no staff. I'm kept quite busy with the usual jobs you get as an enquiry agent.'

'What does your wife think about that? She was never very happy about you being in the police.'

Hardwick took a long swig from his glass before he answered. 'Joan died five years ago, Ralph.'

'Oh, I am sorry to hear that, Bruce. She always looked so fit and youthful. What was it?'

'She had breast cancer. Unfortunately she had it for a long time before it was diagnosed. There wasn't much that could be done for her and she suffered a great deal in the final weeks of her life. But if you don't mind, I'd rather not dwell on that. I'm trying to move on and make a new life on my own.'

'I quite understand, Bruce. I shan't say anything to Jill

about it until after you've left. Now, are you ready for another Scotch? I want to hear more about the work you're doing.'

'Yes on both counts. I'm not driving myself and I can ring for a taxi as soon as you want to throw me out. And before I go I'd like to hear more about what you've been doing since I retired from the force.'

'That's fine then' Ralph said, as he refilled their glasses.

'I recently saw on the news that you had a double murder to deal with. How's it going with that?'

'Not as well as I would like.'

'If you don't mind telling me, what's the problem?'

'I don't mind you knowing, Bruce. You might have some helpful suggestions to make. Between you and me there are too many suspects, and as far as we've been able to discover, they all have the same motive.'

'So, what is their motive?'

Braddock drew a deep breath and then launched into a full explanation of what his detectives had found out from their enquiries.

'From what you say about the methods of carrying out the murders, I can't imagine that your average investor would carry out such revenge for losing money on a poor investment,' replied Hardwick. 'Shares rise and fall all the time and experienced investors take it in their stride. Have you got any wild card investors, who, for example, invested their life savings in the hope of raising sufficient money to ensure a comfortable retirement?'

'It's a rather strange coincidence that you should suggest that, Bruce, because we do have a suspect who fits that profile. However, after our enquiries into his background, a failed identification parade and what seems to have been an obvious frame-up to point to him as the murderer, we have eliminated him from our enquiries.'

They both emptied their glasses before continuing, and Ralph refilled them.

'So, Bruce, what does the best DCI I ever worked under think about that?'

'I think you have a very intriguing problem to solve. From what you've told me it would appear that perhaps one of the high-losing investors hired a killer to murder Stratton and Rackman and then arranged a frame-up for whoever seemed to be the most likely suspect.'

'I like your analysis, Bruce. But what you have done is create a large number of suspects who wanted revenge, but lacked the stomach or skill to have committed the murders and hired a killer to do the job and then frame the man who had the motive and capability to kill.'

'Of course, there is another scenario, which could eliminate those suspects.'

'Okay, Holmes, enlighten me.'

'Let's just suppose, Watson, that the man who was your prime suspect actually carried out the murders and then created a frame-up of himself, which could be easily broken.'

'Well, you've certainly given me something else to think about. I wish we were working together again.'

'So do I, Ralph, but I'm past my best and happier enough with what I'm doing now.'

'Well, let's have one for the road, Holmes.'

'What an excellent suggestion, my dear Watson.'

Braddock filled their glasses while Hardwick used his mobile phone to call a taxi. They had just finished their drinks when the taxi driver rang the doorbell. Braddock followed Hardwick to the door and helped him on with his raincoat. They exchanged goodnights and promises to keep in touch.

# CHAPTER TWENTY-SEVEN

Back home in his near luxury apartment a stone's throw from Barkston Wood golf course, Hardwick read the file Sharon Tate had given him. He could see from its contents how Arkwright had been convinced that Carson was responsible for the murder of Lance Rackman and Roland Stratton. His conviction was supported by Sharon's statement to the police that she had heard Carson threatening Stratton. To Hardwick this was very flimsy evidence and had probably been overstated to the police. It had been established that many of the investors had lost large sums of money when the Linduana Copper Mining Company had crashed, which had, no doubt, caused them to voice their displeasure with the Arkwright and Partners' brokerage.

Thinking about the conversations he had had with Braddock that evening, he reasoned that it was very likely that Braddock's senior detectives held mixed views regarding Carson being the likely killer. His theorizing about the case with Braddock would probably have added complexity to the case. A fresh mind was needed, and he decided to put some time in on checking Carson's alibis for the times of the murders and making his own checks on Carson's background. But all that could wait until tomorrow. He put the file into his briefcase and went to his bedroom.

\*\*\*

Hardwick was an early riser and had shaved and showered by 7 am. He listened to the early morning news over a breakfast of coffee, porridge and marmalade-covered toast. After breakfast he left the clearing up to be done by his cleaner, who arrived at 9 am. She spent two hours every Monday to Friday morning cleaning the apartment, making his bed and washing and ironing his clothes and bed linen.

Before leaving his apartment he wrote a few notes in a pocket book. He read through the notes and then, satisfied with what he had written, he rang for a taxi. He rarely used his own car to drive around London. He'd had enough of that when he had been a serving police officer.

He directed the taxi driver to a small printing shop a couple of miles from his home. Entering the shop, he asked the young woman attending the reception desk if he might have a word with the manager. She went through a door at the rear of the reception area and returned with a black-haired, thickset and fashionably bearded middle-aged man.

The man smiled as he recognized his most regular customer. 'Good morning Mr Hardwick. What can we do for you today?'

'Hello, Josh. I'd like a few business cards made up from

these notes, as soon as you can get them printed,' Hardwick said. He tore a page from his pocket book and handed it to Josh.

Josh read through the notes and grinned. 'If you don't mind waiting in my office with a cup of coffee and today's Guardian, I can get the printing done in about an hour,' he said with a wink.

'That's splendid service. That's a rare thing these days, Josh.'

Josh led Hardwick to his office and told the receptionist to make him a coffee and give him the newspaper to read while he waited for his printing to be done. Then Josh went away to organize the printing. True to his word, he returned within the hour with a card box containing about fifty printed cards.

Hardwick examined the cards. 'These are fine, Josh. How much do I owe you?'

'For you, twenty quid will do.'

'No it won't, Josh,' Hardwick replied, handing him a fifty-pound note.

'Thanks a lot, Mr Hardwick, and cheerio until I see you again,' he said with a wink.

'Ta ta for now, Josh.'

Back home, Hardwick checked the file and turned to the pages containing the names and addresses of all the investors who had invested in the Linduana Copper Mining Company. Robert Carson's name and address was underlined in red. The best time to call on him would be early evening. He would need to use my own car.

Carson was watching an ancient episode of "Columbo", the indefatigable American detective who never failed to solve his homicide cases, when the doorbell rang. He rose reluctantly and went to his front door. He opened the door to see on the front step a tall, grey-haired, middle-aged man wearing an army officer's raincoat. Carson looked at him questioningly.

'You're not selling anything, are you?' he said.

The man smiled. 'Good evening, Mr Carson. No, I'm not selling anything. I'm your area SSAFA representative.' He produced a business card and handed it to Carson. Carson read it, noting that the man's name was Laurence Tarrington and that he was a retired major.

'I'm pleased to make your acquaintance, Major Tarrington, but I can't for the life of me understand why you're calling on me.'

'If you'll invite me in, I'll be happy to explain why I'm here.'

'Yes, please come in, Major. Whatever you're here for makes no difference. I live a fairly lonely life and to talk to an ex-military man will, I'm sure, prove pleasurable.'

Carson fully opened the door and led Tarrington into the sitting room.

'Would you like to take your raincoat off, Major?'

'Yes please, and you can stop calling me Major. Larry will do. Your name is Robert, isn't it?

'Yes, but I answer to Bob.'

Carson took his raincoat and hung it on the hallstand. Returning to the sitting room, Carson saw that Tarrington seemed to be inspecting the room.

'You seem to have organized yourself, Bob.'

'Yes, army life helps one settle anywhere. Take a seat, Larry and tell me why you've called on me.'

'It's simply this. SSAFA have a duty of care for all ex-servicemen and their families, and to help them settle down in civilian life after many years in the service. Now we have been notified that you recently lost your wife and that you are living alone with no relatives near you. We would like to help in any way we can to improve your life. I see you're well housed and seem well able to maintain your accommodation. Do you get anyone in to help with cleaning, laundry or cooking?'

'No, I don't need any help. The cleaning is no problem. As to laundry, there's a reasonably priced laundry a few hundred yards down the road. They wash and dry your clothing and linen and iron it. I do little cooking. I manage with cereals for breakfast, fish and fruit for lunch and a one-course evening meal in a local restaurant.'

'My word, you do lead a rather simple life. What do you do for entertainment?'

'I watch television documentaries and old films and read a lot.'

'So you don't get out very much?'

'No, but I do occasionally visit a theatre or cinema and the local British Legion club.'

'The British Legion, yes that must be a good place for you to meet old comrades.'

'Actually, very few of the former members of my regiment use the local branch.'

'Hmm, so it would be in order to say that you have a very lonely and lacklustre life, Bob,'

'I'm afraid that's true, but it is something I'm obliged to accept, because I have no job and I'm trying to save every penny I can to finance my emigration to Australia, where my daughter and grandchildren live.'

'Oh, so you're planning to leave the country?'

'Yes, when I can raise sufficient money to be accepted as a migrant in Australia and pay for my son-in-law to arrange for the building of an extension to his bungalow.'

'But surely your army long-service terminal grant and pension should be enough to cover those expenses?'

'Yes, they would have been, but I lost most of my terminal grant when I was conned by a smarmy investment consultant to invest in an over-rated prospect, which turned out to be an incompetent fly-by-night African copper mining company, which crashed. The brokerage I invested with would do nothing to try to recover money that had been embezzled by the copper company's chief executive officer.'

'What bad luck, and no doubt a great disappointment for your family,' Tarrington said with contrived sympathy.

'I'll say it was a disappointment, and with everything that was going wrong with my life it was a disaster. I have to admit, I felt like wringing Rackman's neck. But some other very disappointed investor must have stabbed him to death. Or, perhaps Rackman was the victim of an attack by a burglar, as has been suggested.'

'Yes, I remember that case, Bob. The firm's general manager was also murdered. Strangled, I believe.'

'Yes, that's what I heard. It would seem that if it was one man who killed both of these men he must be must be a total nutcase.'

'So you don't consider that your nutcase killer had any justification to kill?'

'No, Larry, not if his justification simply amounted to taking revenge against those responsible for the loss of his investment.'

'But you did say that you felt like wringing Rackman's neck.'

'Yes, but when you're very angry with someone, you often say things you don't mean.'

'Yes, I quite understand. I agree. But tell me Bob, if you don't mind, have you ever killed anyone?'

'Yes, of course, in battle, and I wouldn't be here now if I hadn't in the many wars I've survived.'

'I could ask you the same question, Major.'

'No. Perhaps I've been lucky to have survived 30 years in the Army Intelligence Corps without having to kill anyone.'

'Then you were extremely lucky. Now I feel sure that after all our chin wagging, you probably feel as dry as I do. Can I offer you something to drink - tea, coffee, or whatever you fancy?'

'Yes, Bob I'd like that. I usually have a Scotch during the evening, but better make it coffee, I'm driving tonight.'

Carson went into the kitchen to make a pot of coffee and laid up a tray with all that was necessary and a plate of biscuits. Returning to the sitting room, he saw Tarrington studying his wall-mounted photographs of him in uniform in several war zones.

'You certainly got around when you were in the army, Bob.'

'Yes, I certainly did.' Carson set the tray down on the sofa table.

'I was most interested to see from that framed citation that you were awarded the military cross for bravery in Iraq.'

Carson didn't reply, but busied himself pouring. They

drank their coffee and ate most of the biscuits without much conversation other than about the weather and the various violent incidents that occurred almost daily somewhere in the world.

'Well, Bob, I have to say you make a great cup of coffee. I must be off now, but don't hesitate to call me if you require any kind of assistance. You have my mobile number on the card I gave you. I don't use my landline much because I'm out most of the time visiting chaps like you.'

Carson followed Hardwick to the door and passed his raincoat to him. 'I can't think of anything you can do for me at the moment, but thanks for your engaging company this evening. I hope that when you've nothing better to do you'll call again. Goodnight, Larry.'

'Be assured, Bob, I'll look into what SSAFA can do to help you to join your family in Australia. Goodnight, Bob.'

After Tarrington had gone, Carson poured himself a large whisky and meditated over what he had said during the evening. He certainly had a very engaging and friendly manner and aside from his work for SSAFA, being about the same age and a former soldier, he might be worth cultivating as a friend. His manner of questioning did sometimes make him come across like a policeman, but his service in the Intelligence Corps, when a lot of his time would have been spent questioning enemy prisoners of war, could explain this.

Well satisfied with the evening, Carson finished his whisky and went to bed.

# CHAPTER TWENTY-EIGHT

Carson and Hurst were sitting chatting and drinking in the British Legion Club.

'I had an unexpected visit from an SSAFA representative a couple of evenings ago,' Carson said, for something to talk about.

'What was he, one of those ex-senior officer do-gooders who like to delve into your past history and shoot the line about theirs and then promise to sort out all your problems?'

'On the contrary, he was a very engaging chap. He was a retired major who had served for 30 years in the Intelligence Corps. We had a long conversation about my problems and he assured me that he would do whatever he could to improve my lifestyle. Not once did he talk about his own army career.'

'What was his name?'

'Major Laurence Tarrington,' Carson replied and showed Tarrington's card to Hurst.

Hurst shook his head. 'No, I don't recall ever meeting him. But then why should I? Those intelligence buggers don't spend as much of their time at the sharp end of the business as we did.'

'No, that's true, but there's no doubt that the intelligence reports they produced for field commanders saved many lives.'

'Yeah, but it's a pity there wasn't an intelligence bod available to interview my prisoner. If there had been I might still be in the army and holding a warrant rank.'

'Yes Roger, there was a strong likelihood that if you hadn't gone overboard with that prisoner things would have turned out much better for you. I'm afraid life can be like that. You foul up once, or something happens to suddenly change your circumstances and your whole life can be changed forever.'

Hurst drained his glass. 'Are you ready for another?'

'Yes, why not, I can't think of a better suggestion,' Carson replied and drained his glass. Hurst took their glasses to the bar. 'Two refills please, Charlie.'

Charlie poured the drinks and Hurst dropped a ten-pound note on the bar. 'Keep the change, Charlie.'

Hurst placed the glasses on their table and sat down.

'Now, what were we talking about, Bob?'

'I was simply making a point about how your life can be changed by a single act, whether it's right or wrong. Your life changed drastically when you were court-martialled and dishonourably discharged.'

'Yes, and I lost my pension and my wife divorced me.'

'I'm really sorry about that Roger, but you seem to have got over your problems and you're now enjoying life, I believe.'

'Yeah, I suppose I am better off now. My boss has just given me a rise. By the way, have you thought any more about joining my firm?'

'No, Roger, but the extra money would be a help in getting me to Australia. I'll keep it in mind.'

'You've certainly had your share of bad luck since you came out of the army.'

'Yes, I certainly have, but I don't want to dwell on my misfortunes, so let's talk about something more agreeable. Do you fancy joining me in seeing a well-reviewed stage play or a so-called blockbuster film?'

'Yeah, why not. Have you got any suggestions?'

'*The Imitation Game* is showing at the Vue Cinema in Stratford. I wouldn't describe it as a blockbuster but it's a well-reviewed film, which is based on the true British wartime coup about the cracking of the German Enigma Code machine.'

'Hmm, that sounds worth seeing. What day do you suggest?'

'A late afternoon on a Saturday would suit me, Roger.'

'Yeah, that suits me fine. There's an evening showing at about 7.30 to 8 pm. I suggest we meet at about six.'

'It's a date then. I suggest we have an evening meal before the film, if there's a restaurant near the cinema. Are you familiar with any of the restaurants in the area?'

'Yes, there are three good ones in the cinema - the Southern Terrace, the Balcony and the Loft. Take your pick.'

'Well, as I've never eaten in any of them, I'll let you decide.'

'The Southern Terrace is my favourite so we'll make it there, OK?'

'Yes, but I insist that the meal and the cinema tickets are on me.'

'OK, thanks.' Hurst drained his glass. 'Are you ready for another one?'

'Not really, I want to get a letter written to my daughter for posting in the morning, so if you don't mind I'll slide off home now. Do you want to share a taxi?'

'No, I think I'll stay here until Charlie closes the bar. Goodnight, Bob.'

'I'll see you Saturday evening then. Goodnight, Roger, goodnight Charlie,' Carson said as he walked out of the bar room. He took out his new mobile phone to telephone for a taxi.

# CHAPTER TWENTY-NINE

'Mr Hardwick is here to see you, sir, shall I bring him up?' Sharon said on the internal telephone.

'Yes, as quick as you can, Sharon,' Arkwright replied, his tone conveying his eagerness to hear Hardwick's report.

Sharon led Hardwick up to the first floor and tapped on Arkwright's door.

'Enter!' Arkwright called out loudly.

Sharon and Hardwick entered and waited for Arkwright's response.

'Take a seat, Mr Hardwick. Sharon, you will not be required. I'll call you when Mr Hardwick is leaving.'

As soon as Sharon closed the door, Arkwright leaned forward and looked directly at Hardwick. 'Well, what have you learnt from your interview with Carson?'

'Nothing that suggests to me that he is the man we're after. I interviewed him at length in the guise of a SSAFA representative and found him to be straightforward and in no way intimidated by my questioning. I have to say that unless some direct evidence can be found to link him to the two murders, we are wasting our time.'

'It's my time and I'm paying for yours, Hardwick, so I want you to keep making further enquiries. I'm sure in my own mind that he is guilty. Is there no way you can check his alibis for the times of the killings?'

'To do that would mean me having to drop my SSAFA guise and lose his trust in me as someone looking out for his interests. Anyway, I'm sure the police have already satisfied themselves that he was where he stated he was at the time of the murders.'

'Then keep him under surveillance, tap his phone, follow him, even get into his house, if you can. If you do that I'm sure you'll find something to prove his guilt.'

'Do I have to remind you Albert, that I am not a policeman any more, but a private enquiry agent and for me to tap his phone or break into his house would be criminal? Even pukka police officers would require a magistrate's warrant to do what you're asking. And to get a warrant they would have to convince the magistrate that they had good cause to have one.'

'Very well Bruce, do what you can do without breaking any laws. Visit him again as a SSAFA agent. Talk to him long enough and he might slip up. Take every opportunity to have a sneaky look for the Rolex that was stolen from Rackmans' body. Carson might even start to wear it if he thinks he is no longer a suspect.'

'OK, Albert, I'll give it a few more days and then I must return to other outstanding cases I'm working on.'

'Right, we'll leave things like that then, but I promise

you a handsome bonus if you can get the goods on Carson. I'll get Sharon to take you down now.'

Hardwick stood up and waited until Sharon came to show him out.

'Goodbye, Albert. I'll call back as soon as I have something worth reporting, otherwise I'll see you in three days' time to submit my account.'

'Do your best, Bruce. Goodbye for now.'

# CHAPTER THIRTY

'Is that SSAFA Headquarters?'

'Yes, sir, how may we help you?'

'I'm trying to contact one of your representatives. His name is Laurence Tarrington. He's a retired major.'

'What is your name, sir?'

'Jack Kilroy.'

'Please hold the line while I check for you, Mr Kilroy.'

Hurst sat back in his armchair. He was now in for a long wait and there was no music to listen to. He started to whistle: *This is a lovely way to spend an evening, can't think of anything I'd rather do...* but he stopped when the operator came back on the line. 'I'm afraid we have no one by that name employed by SSAFA. Are you sure you've got the right name?'

'It would seem not,' Hurst said and replaced the receiver.

***

Hardwick sat in his car across the road from where Carson lived and waited. It was around nine o'clock on a Friday morning. Hardwick reasoned that Carson would leave his house sometime during that day, to shop, visit a friend, to go the British Legion Club or simply go out for a walk.

Hardwick had provisioned himself with a lunch box of ham sandwiches, a tin of fruit sweets, a large flask of coffee and two bottles of water. He was listening to the car's radio through a connecting earpiece.

The morning hours crawled by without any sight of Carson. At midday, he ate some of his sandwiches and drank coffee. As he was placing his flask under his seat there was a rap on his car window. He looked up to see a traffic warden peering into the car. Hardwick wound down the window. 'Is there something wrong?' he said politely.

'Yes, there is, sir. You can't park here, this is a restricted area. If you were a disabled driver with a Blue Badge you could park here for a maximum of three hours.'

'Oh dear, I am very sorry, officer. I am disabled, but I've forgotten to put my disabled driver badge on show,' Hardwick said in an obsequious tone. He reached into his dashboard compartment and withdrew a Blue Badge card, a forgery which had been created by one of the dubious cronies he had used for illegal purposes after leaving the police service. He handed it to the traffic warden, who checked the details and compared the photograph with Hardwick's face.

'How long have you been here, Mr Hardwick?'

'I arrived a few minutes before you came, officer.'

'Then you should have set the clock card to the time you came.'

'I sincerely apologize for being so absent-minded, officer.'

'I'll not give you a ticket this time, but make sure your blue badge is properly displayed in future.'

'Yes, I promise, officer,' Hardwick replied, tongue in cheek.

An hour later Carson came out of his house carrying an empty linen bag and headed towards the town's main shopping area. Hardwick waited until Carson was about fifty yards away before buttoning his car coat and putting on a woollen scarf and a corduroy cap, which he pulled down over his eyes. He followed Carson, keeping fifty yards behind him. Carson entered a bakery. Hardwick stopped to gaze into a shop window until Carson emerged, having bought at least one large loaf. He next entered a newsagent's. Hardwick again stopped to look into a shop window. Carson came out of the shop with a large newspaper showing at the top of his bag. A Telegraph or Guardian reader, Hardwick thought.

Carson's next stop was at a small but smart "breakfast all day" café. Hardwick crossed the road and glanced towards the café. He could see Carson ordering a meal. While he was waiting to be served he was drinking tea or coffee and reading his newspaper.

Hardwick had hoped that his surveillance of Carson's movements might be more fruitful. He was disappointed, and felt that it had been a waste of time. Perhaps Arkwright had been right when he suggested that if there was any evidence to be found of Carson's involvement in the murders, it might be in his house. He decided that he would return the following day and gain access when it was likely Carson would be out shopping or having a meal out.

\*\*\*

The following morning at 10 o'clock, Hardwick drove to Carson's address and parked opposite. He displayed his Blue Badge on the top of his dashboard and set it at the time of his arrival. His intention was to move the time forward every half hour while he was waiting for Carson to appear.

At a few minutes past two o'clock Carson came walking back from the direction of town, carrying two laden shopping bags. He must have gone out before I arrived, thought Hardwick. It was Saturday, so surely he was going out somewhere this evening, perhaps to the British Legion Club, if not for a meal, or to spend an evening in a local pub. He would wait until about six and then go.

At precisely five o'clock Carson came out of his house and stood at the kerb. He must be waiting for a taxi. Hardwick noted that he was smartly dressed in a dark lounge suit and was wearing a tie - probably his regimental one - and carrying an umbrella. He looked as though he was out for the evening, which suited Hardwick's plan to enter his house.

Two minutes later the taxi arrived and Carson was driven off to where he was going. Hardwick waited a minute or two before getting out of his car and approaching Carson's front door. He looked around to see if anyone was in sight who might see him entering the house. Hardwick was well equipped to open most conventional door locks, and within seconds he had unlocked the door and was inside the house.

From his long experience as a detective he was aware of the most likely places for criminals to hide items that could be used as evidence against them. He wasted no time in checking them all. If he found the Rolex watch, that should clinch Carson's guilt, unless of course, someone was trying to frame Carson.

He first checked the toilet cistern and the bathroom cabinet, and found nothing that didn't belong in them. He opened all the suitcases and travel bags he found on the bottom of the wardrobe floor. All were empty. Next he started on the chest of drawers from the bottom drawer up in the master bedroom. Without disturbing the neatly-folded shirts and underclothes, he felt for any foreign objects. There were none. The top drawer contained neatly rolled-up socks. There was nothing hidden in them.

He went into the sparsely-furnished second bedroom and found that the wardrobe and all the drawers were empty. He checked every drawer and cupboard in the well-ordered kitchen. His search revealed nothing but the fact that Carson kept his home, clean, tidy and well maintained.

As he entered the hall he realized that he hadn't checked the drawer attached to the hallstand. He opened the drawer, which seemed to only contain a few handbills advertising take away or home delivery of Indian, Chinese and Italian meals. He pulled the drawer right out and nearly dropped it in surprise. A Rolex gold watch was stuck to the back of the drawer with Blu-Tack.

He prised it off and peeled the Blu-Tack off the back of the watch, wrapped it in his handkerchief and put it in his inside jacket pocket. Time for some careful consideration regarding the unexpected discovery of Rackman's watch, he thought, as he left the house and returned to his car to drive home in haste. Back home, he removed his car coat, hat and scarf and took the watch out of his jacket pocket and laid it out on his handkerchief on the sofa table. He made some strong coffee and poured a double measure of brandy into the cup.

He sipped his coffee as he looked at the watch. Of all the places in his house that Carson could have used for hiding the watch, he had chosen to put it in the hallstand drawer. That didn't make sense. It suggested a very clever little frame-up. A casual visitor to the house would hardly have the opportunity to look for a hiding place, but he could take advantage of the drawer when he put his top coat on the hallstand. The fact that Blu-Tack had been used to hold the watch at the back of the drawer suggested that that the action had been planned. If the police had decided to make a thorough search of the house it would probably have been found, which would certainly have put Carson up Queer Street.

Now what should he do about the watch? If he showed it to Arkwright he would be delighted and would see that the police were immediately advised. If he took it to the police, they would be interested in knowing how he had obtained it. No, if he could find out from Carson who had visited him since he had moved in he might be able to nail the real killer. That being the case, he could probably persuade the police that he had found it by accident when he had been placing his gloves in the drawer.

Having decided what he would do next, Hardwick finished his second cup of fortified coffee, returned the handkerchief-wrapped Rolex to his jacket pocket and went to bed.

# CHAPTER THIRTY-ONE

It was Sunday morning, so Hardwick stayed in bed until 9 am, thinking about what he intended doing that day. After shaving and completing his ablutions, he dressed in a smart dark grey suit, white shirt and a Intelligence Corps tie, which he had purchased through the British Legion on-line shop. He made a breakfast of porridge, toast and marmalade and strong tea.

At 10 am he telephoned Carson. It was a minute or two before he answered the telephone.

'Hello,' he said, 'who's calling me at this time on a Sunday?'

'Good morning, Bob. It's Laurence Tarrington. I hope I haven't caught you at a bad time.'

'Not at all, Larry, I was in the bathroom. I had rather a late night and didn't get up at my usual time.'

Hardwick gave a little laugh. 'That's what retirement is all about, Bob. Take it easy. There's no more rise and shine to go on parade for you. The reason I'm calling is to check that all is well with you and to ask if you would have any objection to me coming over later today to talk about your problems?'

'Yes, feel free to call at any time. I'm rarely out of the house. But I managed a night out for dinner and a film show last night.'

'Splendid, you should do that more often. What did you see?'

'*The Imitation Game*. It's a great film, based on the true story of how the German Enigma Code machine was solved. We both enjoyed it.'

'So you had company then?'

'Yes, I went with a former member of my regiment.'

'That must have been a nice change for you.'

'Yes, it was. Now about your visit, I'm about to grab a quick breakfast, which will be over before eleven. So you can come at any time after that.'

'Good, then you can expect me at about 11.30, okay?'

'That's fine, see you then.'

Carson's doorbell rang at 11.35. He answered the door and admitted Hardwick, who removed his topcoat and hung it on the hallstand; as he did so he noted Carson's composed expression.

Carson led Hardwick into the sitting room. Hardwick sat on the sofa and Carson sat in his favourite chair facing him.

'Is there anything I can get you, Larry?'

'Not just now, Bob, perhaps later when I've told you what I've been doing to see if I can help you to join your family. I've looked into the matter of getting you a financial grant. I've received no decision about this yet, but I feel sure that there should be a favourable response in the near future. Of course SSAFA will want to know all about your financial situation before they finally decide what amount they can grant you.'

'Yes, I know all about how these things work. In the meantime I'm saving whatever I can to add to the money I have in the bank.'

'Good, you have the right idea. But all that aside, I have to say I'm very concerned about your lonely lifestyle. Loneliness can be very depressing, even harmful, as you approach old age.'

'Yes, I do miss my wife, we were so happy together. When I was away with the battalion I never felt lonely. There was always plenty to keep me occupied.'

'Well perhaps it's just as well that you have found an old comrade to spend some time with. I'd like to bet that you don't have many callers to see you.'

'You're right there, Larry. But I did get two last week. They came to read the gas and electric meters,' Carson replied with a laugh.

'What about your old army chum, doesn't he ever call?'

'Oh him, yes he's been here once or twice, but I have to confess I don't really think of him as a chum. We've nothing much more in common than that we were once in the same battalion in the army. I suppose I'm using him as a sort of makeshift pal.'

'Does he think of you in the same way?'

'Well, he's got no friends that I'm aware of and his wife divorced him some time ago, so I expect he feels much the same way about me - just a makeshift friend.'

'I'd have thought that you both being in the same regiment you would have had a lot in common. From what you say about him being friendless and divorced, he seems to be in a pretty lonely state. Perhaps I should go to see him to try to improve his lifestyle.'

'Before you do that, Larry, I think you ought to know a little of his history. He was a platoon sergeant in our battalion and I was the battalion sergeant major, about 12 years older than him. So, you can see that there was a gulf of age and rank between us. We were engaged in the war with Iraq and we had a brief but bloody battle in which Sergeant Roger Hurst lost two members of his platoon. His platoon commander was wounded and the senior NCO of the Iraqi platoon, which had fought Hurst's platoon, was captured. Hurst took it upon himself to question the soldier about the whereabouts of his battalion position. The soldier refused to give more than his number, rank and name. Hurst then beat him nearly to death without obtaining the information he wanted. I intervened and Hurst was placed under arrest to await trial by field general court martial. His only defence was that there was no field intelligence officer, or NCO, available to question the prisoner and he felt that it was imperative, and his responsibility, to find out the strength and position of the enemy battalion as soon as possible.

'He was found guilty, sentenced to be stripped of his rank and awarded a long period of detention. On his release from the detention barracks he was discharged with ignominy. As a result he lost his right to a pension and his wife divorced him.'

'Bloody hell, Bob! Excuse my French, but I have to say I

feel truly sorry for the poor bugger. I think he needs the help of SSAFA more than you do. And from what you say, he seems not to bear any grudge against you for being a witness for the prosecution at his court martial. If you can give me his address I'll go and see him as soon as I can.'

Carson reached into a drawer in the sideboard and took out his address book. 'That's his address,' he said opening the book at the "H" page.

Tarrington took out his notebook and copied the address into it. 'Yes, I know the address. It's in a rather seedy area of North Woolwich. I wouldn't want to leave my car on the roadside there at night. Would you have any objection to me bringing him here so that I could try to firm up your relationship with him?'

'Not at all, Larry, if you think it will do any good. We seem to get on well enough and I've got no other friends living in this area.'

'Right, I'll give him a ring and suggest he comes here with me when it's convenient for you.'

'He works during the week, so I expect he'd prefer to come on a weekday evening. Any evening would suit me. Just give me a ring, Larry, and I'll make sure I'm going to be in.'

'Well thanks for all the information you've given me about Roger. I'll be in touch as soon as I can arrange a meeting here.'

Carson accompanied him to the front door and watched him walking to his car. He waved as Tarrington drove off.

\*\*\*

As soon as he got home, Hardwick rang Hurst.

'Hello,' Hurst answered.

'Good evening Mr Hurst, we haven't met before. My name is Laurence Tarrington and I'm the SSAFA representative for North London and Essex.'

'Oh, yeah, so why are you ringing me?'

'I am providing advice and support for one of your former army comrades, a Mr Robert Carson. He tells me that you have had your share of misfortunes and that you have recently developed a friendly relationship with him to combat the loneliness you are both enduring. He tells me he doesn't have any friends living anywhere near him. He also said that he had an enjoyable evening in your company last night and...'

'What's all this leading to?' Hurst interrupted.

'Simply this. I suggested to him that we should all get together to see what can be done to improve your lifestyles. He agreed that we might all meet at his home for one evening. So I'm hoping you will agree to what I'm suggesting.'

'Yeah, why not? I'd be quite happy to have an evening with old Bob and you to talk about any financial or other assistance SSAFA can provide for two old soldiers. I'm free tomorrow evening, if that's OK with you and Bob. My car is having an MOT at present, so can you pick me up from my home? Perhaps we can have a little chat about my personal problems on the way to Bob's place.'

'Certainly, Roger, that's a good idea. What time do you suggest?'

'I could be waiting outside the block of flats where I live at six pm. You've got my address, I suppose, Mr Tarrington?'

'Yes, Bob gave it to me. By the way, never mind the Mr

Tarrington, I like to keep my relationships with my SSAFA clients to be informal, so just call me Larry.'

'Okay, Larry, I'll be waiting outside at six' Hurst said, and put down the receiver.

Hardwick then rang Carson to confirm the arrangements to meet at his home at about seven o'clock the following evening.

***

Hardwick left his home at 5 pm and managed to avoid most of the heavy commuter traffic, arriving at Hurst's address at 5.50. As he pulled to a stop in front of the tower block, Hurst stepped out of the shadows and walked to Hardwick's car. He was wearing a raincoat, a woollen scarf, a check patterned cap and gloves.

'Good evening, Roger, welcome aboard,' Hardwick said as he opened the car door from the inside.

'Hi, Larry you made good time, it's just five minutes to six.'

'Yes, my army training made me very time conscious. You must know the drill, if you have to be somewhere at a particular time you should be there five minutes early.'

Hurst fastened his seat belt and Hardwick put the car into gear and moved off.

'So you were in the army, Larry. What was your regiment?'

'I served for thirty years in the Intelligence Corps.'

'So, I suppose you were in a lot of war zones during that time.'

'Yes, quite few, but I thought you wanted to chat to me about your background.'

'Yes, that's right, but when you said you had been in the army, I was naturally curious about your service. Did you ever serve in Iraq or Afghanistan?'

'Yes, but I was always way behind the line at Divisional Headquarters, studying field intelligence reports.'

'Oh, so you were a commissioned officer then.'

'Yes, I finished up as a major. But that's enough about me. Let me hear about your problems. Bob Carson has told me something about your past history, but I'd like to hear about it from you.'

'Okay, Larry, but I'm afraid I must ask you to stop at the next pub so that I can have a piss. I've a weak bladder. I shouldn't have had a second mug of tea before I left home.'

'That's all right, Roger, just hold your water, we'll soon find somewhere for you to have your pee.'

A minute later Hardwick pulled up outside a public house. Hurst undid his seat belt, got out of the car and walked into the pub. He came out a few minutes later and crossed the deserted street to the car. As he entered the car his right hand came out of his raincoat pocket holding a lead-filled cosh, which he smashed down on Hardwick's bare head.

'Take that, you lying bastard!' he grunted. 'You were no more in the Intelligence Corps than I'm a Victoria Cross holder,' he said. Then he struck Hardwick on the head again.

Hurst undid Hardwick's safety belt and pulled him over to the passenger's seat. Searching Hardwick's clothing, he removed his mobile phone, wallet and a notebook. Better

take that, he thought, it might include his address. He then
went around to the other side of the car, got into the driver's
seat and drove until he came to the outskirts of a small town
on the banks of the River Thames. He drove along the road,
which ran parallel with the bank of the river, and turned
the car to face the river. Next he released the handbrake,
got out of the car and shut the door. Going to the rear of the
vehicle, he pushed it until it began to move under its own
momentum. He watched the car roll down the bank and
drop into the fast-flowing river.

Hurst stood on the bank and watched the stream of air
bubbles coming from the car as it sank out of sight. Then he
walked the half mile or so to the centre of the town whistling
*'This is a lovely way to spend an evening, can't think of
anything I'd rather do...'* and waited at a bus stop for a bus
that would take him back to North Woolwich.

Back home, Hurst poured a large whisky and drank it
straight down. Now to establish an alibi. He telephoned
Carson.

'Hey, Bob, what's going on? It's after eight and there's
no sign of your tame SSAFA representative. He said he'd
pick me up from here at six. Is he with you?'

'No, I expected you both to be here before seven. I rang
him at about 7.45, but there was no answer. The only reason
I could think for him not arriving at your place is that he
had been called out to some sort of military family
emergency.'

'Yes, I think you're right there, but he might have given
one of us a ring to say there was a change of plan.'

'Hmm, I agree. It seems unlike him to be so remiss. No
doubt he'll get back to us when he's dealt with whatever

stopped him picking you up. If I hear anything from him I'll let you know.'

'I'll do the same, if I hear anything from him. Cheerio, Bob.'

Carson said 'Goodnight,' but Hurst had already replaced his receiver.

***

Wondering why Tarrington had failed to contact either himself or Hurst, Carson had difficulty in getting to sleep that night. When he got up he couldn't wait until 9 am, when he guessed most office staff started work, to give SSAFA Headquarters a call to check the whereabouts of Tarrington.

He first rang Tarrington's number and got no reply. Next he rang SSAFA Headquarters. This time he got an immediate reply. 'Good morning, how may I help you?'

'I'm calling to check if Laurence Tarrington is available. I understand he's your North London and Essex representative.'

'What is your name, sir?'

'Robert Carson. I'm a retired army warrant officer and Major Tarrington had arranged for a meeting at my home with another former soldier. He didn't turn up and never rang either of us to explain why he didn't come to the arranged meeting. I'm a little...'

'This is extraordinary,' the operator interrupted. 'I had another caller asking about someone of that name a few days ago. As I explained to that gentleman, we have no one of that name working for SSAFA.'

'Well, that is strange, because Major Tarrington gave me his business card, which identified him as one of your representatives. He was helping me deal with certain personal problems.

'I'm sorry, sir, but it seems to me that you have been the victim of some sort of a hoax or a scam. If you do need our assistance I can arrange for a genuine representative to contact you.'

'No thank you, not just now, but I'd be interested to know the name of your earlier caller.'

'As far as I can remember his name was Jack Kilroy. He didn't give me any information about himself, and when I told him Laurence Tarrington didn't work for us he rang off without a word.'

'Thank you for your trouble,' Carson said.

'Glad to be of help, Mr Carson. My advice is that this matter should be reported to the police.'

'I probably will do that,' Carson replied.

# CHAPTER THIRTY-TWO

Three days later DCI Warner was conducting a morning briefing attended by Detective Superintendent Braddock. After updating the duty uniformed officers and detectives on current outstanding crimes, Warner produced a report regarding the finding of a car in the River Thames by the police river patrol section the previous day.

He read out the report. It stated that a body had been found in the car and had been identified, through the car's registration number, as Bruce Hardwick. Hardwick's wallet had been removed, so it would seem that he had been the victim of someone who had been given a lift by him and then bludgeoned him to death with some sort of blunt instrument.

'Could his injuries have been sustained when the car went into the river?'

'No, they're consistent with him being struck twice on the back of his head,' Warner said. 'He was probably dead before the car hit the water.'

'Bruce Hardwick murdered, bloody hell!' Braddock almost shouted. 'He was my DCI when I was an inspector. I was only talking to him a few days ago. He told me he was working as a private enquiry agent. Was anything else found on his body?'

'Nothing more than some loose change, a Yale type key, a handkerchief and a comb,' replied Warner.

'No mobile phone, pocket book or diary?' Braddock queried.

'No, boss, but why would he carry a pocket book now that he was no longer a police officer?'

'Old habits die hard, Owen. As a private detective he would have made notes about the cases he was dealing with. This makes me wonder why his killer took the book. Perhaps he was connected to one of Hardwick's cases. I want every man you can spare to work on this case. He was one of us. I will not rest until his killer is found.'

'Are you going to clear it with the Borough Commander, boss? He's been pushing us for more attention to be given to the Rackman and Stratton murders.'

'Yes, of course, but when he learns of the death of one of his borough's former top detectives, he'll be just as anxious as I am to give it high priority.'

'Right, sir, I'll detail a team to get on with it straight away.'

Braddock took Warner's report to the Borough Commander's office. 'You won't have heard about this yet, sir.' He placed the report on Chief Superintendent Alec Patton's desk.

Patton, well past the normal retirement age for the police, but as sharp-eyed as he had ever been, quickly read the report. 'Is this Bruce Hardwick the one-time DCI I heard so much about when I took over the borough?'

'Yes, that's him, sir. I was one of his detective inspectors. He taught me all I know about the job.'

'I take it you want my clearance to launch a full-scale investigation into his murder?'

'Yes, sir, that's exactly what I want.'

'You have it, but our top brass will want to know all about this case, so keep me well-informed, Ralph.'

'I shall, sir.'

'Then away you go, Ralph,' Patton said with a wave of his hand.

Braddock returned to the CID and looked into Warner's office.

'Something we must do straight away. Send DI Ahmed, DS Logan and a couple of DCs to enter Hardwick's flat. I have his address, and the key that was found on his body is probably the one to his front door. Hardwick was a widower and he has no relatives living in the area, so collect all his personal papers, documents and anything else you consider to be in any way of significance or value and bring them here for examination and deposit in the CID Evidence Store.'

DI Ahmed, accompanied by DS Paul Logan, DC Peter Blaydon and DC Jeff Holt, went straight to Hardwick's address and entered his flat.

'Paul, you and Peter search every cupboard and drawer in the two bedrooms and collect all papers, documents and items of apparent value and put them on the dining table,' ordered Ahmed. 'Jeff, you come with me to search the living room, kitchen and bathroom.'

The dining table was soon covered with personal

documents, case files, bank statements, accounts for enquiries made and items of jewellery.

'Paul, I want all these items itemized and bagged,' said Ahmed.

'What about this, guv?' said Logan, holding up a wrist watch. 'It's a Rolex and it looks like it's made of gold. I found it in his bedside locker wrapped in a handkerchief. I think it's a possibility that this is the very watch that was stolen from Rackman.'

'Yes, you may be right. It will have a serial number on it somewhere. Check it and get onto the manufacturers. I'm sure they keep records of the purchasers of their watches. You can also check Rackman's papers to see if it was insured. If it was, the serial number should be on the policy document.'

'From his business cards and other papers it seems ex-DCI Hardwick was working as a private enquiry agent, guv.'

'Yes, there's a lot to be learnt from the papers we've found, so get them bagged and taken back to the office,' answered Ahmed.

Back at the station later that day, Ahmed took the bagged items to DCI Warner's office. Warner looked though the papers and documents and buzzed Braddock for an audience.

'Yes, come up straight away Owen, and bring Ahmed with you,' Braddock replied.

Warner emptied the property bag onto a side table and Braddock looked through the documents and files.

'Well, this lot confirms what Hardwick told me about him working as a private eye,' he said. 'This looks like a very expensive watch to be left in a bedside locker and he wasn't wearing it when he visited me. As I recall he was wearing an Omega.' He was pleased to note that Warner and Ahmed were clearly impressed by his observation. 'I now have a distinct feeling that you are now going to tell me that this was Rackman's Rolex,' he said with a hint of a smile as he picked up the watch.

'Yes, boss. DS Logan has made the necessary checks and it has been confirmed by the manufacturers that the watch was purchased by Lance Rackman,' Warner said.

'The big question now is, how did Hardwick get it?' Braddock said. 'As far as we are aware the only connection he had with the Rackman and Stratton murder case, which is borne out from this case file, is that under the guise of being a SSAFA representative he has been interviewing Robert Carson, one of our suspects in the case. Hardwick's case notes indicate that he considered it is very unlikely that Carson was the killer. I'm inclined to agree with his findings. Something else we need to know - who was Hardwick working for?'

'I'd put my money on Albert Arkwright, sir, the senior partner of the brokerage company that employed Stratton and Rackman,' said Ahmed. 'Arkwright has been very critical about the way we've been handling the case. He's convinced that Carson was responsible for both murders.'

'If you're right, Ahmed, you'd better call on Arkwright,' said Braddock. 'If he was Hardwick's employer he might know something we don't. You can tell him that Hardwick is now dead.'

'Right sir, I'll get onto it first thing in the morning,' Ahmed replied.

# CHAPTER THIRTY-THREE

It was early evening and Carson was engaged in doing the Guardian Quick Crossword when there was a ring at the front door. He put the newspaper down and went to the front door. He opened it to see Hurst standing on the doorstep.

'I hope I haven't come at a bad time for you, Bob, but I thought I'd call in to see how you were and if you had any plans for Christmas week.'

'No, it's not a bad time for me, and no I haven't made any plans for Christmas. Come in and have a drink or two with me,' Carson said, leading Hurst to the sitting room.

'I'll just hang my raincoat up and join you,' Hurst said as he took off his coat. He feigned fumbling as he was hanging it up and let it slip onto the drawer on the hallstand. As he lifted it up, he quietly opened the drawer and slid his hand to the back. He gasped audibly when he found that the Rolex watch was gone.

'Are you all right out there, Roger?' Carson called out.

'Yes, I just had trouble finding the hook, in the half light.'

'Sorry, I should have switched the hall light on.'

Hurst entered the sitting room and saw Carson calmly pouring two glasses of whisky. He must have removed the watch himself. Apart from a couple of meter readers and Tarrington, nobody else had been in there to look into the drawer. Yet Carson was so composed, as if he was unaware of the existence of the watch.

Hurst settled down on the sofa and Carson passed him his drink.

'So, what have you been up to since I last saw you, Roger?'

Hurst nearly choked on his drink. Did Carson know he had put the watch in drawer? Was he just playing with him?

'Sorry for that, Bob, the drink went down the wrong way,' he said.

'That's OK, but why not try sipping your drink rather than gulping it down?'

Hurst reddened and wiped his mouth with the back of his hand. 'I've not been doing very much - just working, eating take-aways, drinking too much and watching television.'

'Has Tarrington been in touch with you with an apology for not showing up?'

'No, he hasn't. Has he phoned you?'

'No, and I think I might have the answer as to why. I rang SSAFA headquarters and was told that they had no one of that name working for them. They also told me that someone by the name of Jack Kilroy had been on to them to ask the same question. I found that to be rather a strange coincidence.'

'It's my opinion, Bob, that he was some sort of confidence trickster. His scam may have been to promise us some sort of grant and he would need our bank account details so that the money could be paid into them. The fact that someone else was checking on him suggests that he may have been another of Tarrington's potential victims.'

'You may be right, Roger, but I have to say that I didn't get that impression of him. And as to me being awarded a grant, I'm not that hard up to need charity. Anyway, if he realizes he's been rumbled, I doubt we'll hear anything more from him. Now what were you hinting at when you asked if I had anything planned for the weekend?'

'Well, it's Christmas next week, so I thought it might be a good idea to go somewhere special for a Christmas blowout. Afterwards we could get a couple of ladies of the night to spend the night with us in a posh London hotel.'

'Yes, that sounds like it might make an enjoyable evening, but I'm not too keen to make the acquaintance of any woman who makes her living in the sex trade. HIV is rife these days and I've no desire to risk contracting it!'

Hurst gave a short laugh. Bob, you are being an old fuddy-duddy! There's very little chance of you catching any nasty disease if you wear a condom. Most prostitutes wouldn't let you near them if you weren't wearing one. They usually provide them anyway.'

'I'm sure you're right, Roger, but since my dear wife died I haven't had any thoughts about sex. So, if you don't mind I'll skip that part of the festivities and do some shopping for Christmas presents for my family in Australia.'

'As you wish, Bob, but I'll make arrangements for two girls to be available in case you change your mind.'

'There's no chance of that, Roger, but I'm sure you'll enjoy the three in the bed routine.'

'I'll make a booking for dinner, breakfast and two double rooms at the Charing Cross Hotel for next Tuesday. We can meet in the hotel bar at six for a few drinks, then dinner at about 7.30. I'll fix it for the girls to report for duty at ten. Is that all right for you?'

'Yes, I'll be there. Now, if you don't mind I've planned to watch a repeat of an old *Colombo* episode.'

'I'll join you with that if there's a chance of another drink,' Hurst responded with alacrity.

Carson gave a deep sigh and poured whisky into their empty glasses.

# CHAPTER THIRTY-FOUR

'There are two police officers here to see you, Mr Arkwright.'

'Have you checked their identities, Sharon?'

'Yes, they're Detective Inspector Ahmed and Detective Sergeant Logan.'

'Then send them up. There's no need for you to accompany them, they know the way.'

DI Ahmed tapped on Arkwright's door.

'Come in!' Arkwright shouted.

Ahmed and Logan entered the office and approached Arkwright's desk. Arkwright stood up and glowered at them. 'What do you want now? I hope you've come to tell me that you've arrested that man Carson.'

'May we sit down please, sir?' Ahmed said politely.

'Yes and get on with what this is all about. I'm a very busy man and haven't got time to listen any more to your pathetic excuses for not making any headway with your investigation into the murder of two of my employees.'

Arkwright sat down and Ahmed and Logan followed suit. Ahmed took a file out of his briefcase and Logan took out a notebook and a biro from his overcoat pocket.

'It has come to our notice that you have hired a private enquiry agent named Bruce Hardwick to investigate the murder of your employees. Is this information factual, sir?'

'Yes, I have, but I can't see that it is of any concern to you.'

'Unfortunately, it is a matter of great concern to us. Bruce Hardwick, a retired detective chief inspector, has been found dead in his car, which was taken from the River Thames. From the medical evidence we have obtained, Mr Hardwick was brutally murdered.'

'Then he's probably another victim of Carson's. He told me he had spoken to Carson and he promised to let me have his final report a couple of days ago. The fact that he is now dead explains why he didn't complete his investigation.'

'Yes, we are aware of that, but there is no evidence that Carson had anything to do with the death of Hardwick. In fact Hardwick introduced himself, under a false name, as a SSAFA representative, and his case file, which has been examined by us, reveals that he considered that Carson was most unlikely to be the murderer.'

'Well I don't give a tinker's cuss what Hardwick considered. I'm writing to the Commissioner of the Metropolitan Police to complain about your negative approach in dealing with this case. I shall, of course, copy my letter to the Home Secretary.'

Ahmed returned the file to his briefcase and stood up. Logan returned his notebook and pen to his overcoat pocket and stood up.

'I have noted your displeasure about our handling of this case, Mr Arkwright, and I shall report the matter to my superior officer. As to your intention to write to the Commissioner and the Home Secretary, that is, of course, your right, but I do assure you that everything possible is being done to bring this case to a satisfactory close. If you have nothing more to say, I bid you good morning.'

Arkwright remained tight-lipped as Ahmed and Logan walked out of his office.

On their way back to their station, Ahmed turned to Logan, who was driving. 'Well Paul, do you still think that Carson is our man?'

'After what poor old Hardwick had to say, I'm beginning to have doubts about who is behind the murders. The case is becoming more baffling as every day goes by.'

'Yes, you're right there. That's why we need analytical detectives to get to the truth rather than those who jump to their conclusions without first giving due consideration to all the facts in the case.'

Logan took the hint. He became very sulky and didn't say another word until they reached the police divisional headquarters. Ahmed went straight to DCI Warner's office and told him about Arkwright's response to Hardwick's murder and his threat to write to the Commissioner and the Home Secretary.

Warner sighed deeply. 'So, it was rather a waste of police time, Samier. But since Arkwright seems convinced that Carson is the killer, you'd better detail one of your team to keep a close watch on the old soldier. But redouble your background checks on all the investors concerned in the crash of that African copper mine company.'

'Right ho boss. If that's all, I'll get on with it.'

'There's nothing else from me, Samier, but I have to say that I'm fast coming to the conclusion that we might be looking for a psychotic killer, motivated by some other reason for the murders.'

# CHAPTER THIRTY-FIVE

Hurst and Carson met at the Charing Cross Hotel at 5 pm that Tuesday. They had one drink in the hotel bar and then split up, Carson to do some Christmas shopping for his family and Hurst to arrange for two female companions to join them at the hotel after they had had dinner, which was planned for 8 pm.

Hurst and Carson returned to the hotel a few minutes before eight and had a drink in the hotel bar before going into the dining room. Neither of them had much to say during the typical Christmas dinner. The meal was finished by 9.30 and Carson excused himself to return to his room to take medication, his excuse for leaving before Hurst's guests arrived.

'Join us in the bar when you've taken your pills,' Hurst said with a laugh. Carson nodded and went to his room.

Hurst went to the bar and waited for Pearl and Ruby,

the two girls he had hired for the evening. They turned up at 9.45 and Hurst ordered champagne cocktails.

'I hope you'll like them,' he said. They both gave little giggles and Pearl said that they were their favourite cocktail.

'I thought you said we were going to meet two gentlemen for the evening,' Ruby said, as she sipped her drink.

'Yes, I did,' Hurst said with a forced smile, 'but I'm afraid my friend was caught short and had to go to his room. He'll be back soon. Anyway, if he doesn't come back we can manage without him, I'm sure.'

The girls giggled and drained their glasses. Hurst ordered more drinks and the girls' mindless chatter continued throughout the evening.

'I don't think you girls are going to be safe returning home alone so late,' Hurst said with a saucy grin. 'You're welcome to share my room.'

'Oh, so you're thinking of rogering us, Roger,' replied Pearl, lowering her eyes.

'Well, isn't that what we're here for, Pearl,' said her friend. 'He looks as though he could manage us both and come up with the right remuneration for our services.' She banged her empty glass on the bar for the tenth time that evening.

Hurst emptied his glass and placed it gently on the bar. 'I think we've all had enough to drink for one evening, so let's now repair to my chamber to find out what pleasures await us.'

Both girls giggled their way to the lift, which took them to Hurst's room.

\*\*\*

Hurst slept in until 9.30 am. Pearl and Ruby had left around 3 am, while their unaware and wearied host had slept on through the night. Hurst went down to the dining room, where he found that Carson was just finishing his breakfast.

After exchanging good mornings, Hurst examined the menu and ordered a full English breakfast, which he attacked with gusto, demonstrating his ability to talk with his mouth full.

'You missed a great night with the girls, Bob. You're not past getting a bit of the other, are you?'

'I've not given the matter much thought lately, Roger, but my absence from the scene enabled you to doubly enjoy the company of your two ladies of the night. For your health's sake I do hope you took appropriate precautions.'

'I always do,' Roger answered with a smirk. 'Anyway, that's enough talk about our sex lives. What's new for you?'

'Before we came away, I went to see Albert Arkwright, the senior partner of that brokerage firm I dealt with. I complained to him that I was getting a lot of attention from the police and put it down to the fact that he was somehow convinced that I had murdered his employees. His response to that was to say that none of his investors could possibly be murderers. Most of them were ex-public school boys and all had successful business careers or were highly-placed officials in national and local government, whereas I was a mere infantry soldier, hired by the government to kill our nation's enemies. He went on to say that I was harassing him and that if I didn't stop he would report the matter to the police and arrange for his solicitor to seek a restraining order.'

'Bloody hell!' Hurst exclaimed, nearly choking on a mouthful of bacon. 'So he's one of those high-falutin' bosses, who think you have to have had a public school or university education to be a person of any value. To him, the likes of us are merely cannon fodder to protect the overseas interests of the likes of him.'

'You put it very strongly, Roger, but I have to agree that in the past returning servicemen who'd put their lives on the line for their country were poorly treated. Thankfully, things are a lot better these days.'

'I know about that, Bob, but you're a holder of the Military Cross for gallantry and you deserve some respect.'

'Forget it, Roger. My main concern at this time is joining my family in Australia.'

'If you're short of money I could lend you enough to pay your fare.'

'Thanks for the offer, Roger. I do have enough money to fly out there, but I shall need a lot more to be accepted as a permanent resident of the country.'

'Have you thought any more about joining my firm as a debt collector?'

'No, not really, Roger. I couldn't see myself doing that job. Perhaps I'm too soft-hearted to badger people into paying back their loans.'

'That's a load of bullshit, Bob. You didn't get to be a sergeant major by being soft-hearted.'

Carson gave a short laugh. 'It's a mystery to me. Anyway, judging by the looks that head waiter is giving us, I think we've overstayed our welcome. You've finished your breakfast at great speed, so I suggest we leave.'

'Yes, I need to be back at work this afternoon and no doubt you'll be parcelling all your Christmas presents up for sending to Aussie.'

They both went to the reception to pay their bills, but Hurst insisted that he settle for both of them. They then returned to their rooms to collect their belongings and leave the hotel to catch their respective trains to take them home.

# CHAPTER THIRTY-SIX

'Good morning. I should like to speak to Mr Arkwright.'

'This is Sharon, Mr Arkwright's personal assistant. Who's calling, please?'

'My name is Jack Kilroy and I should like to consult with him about making investments through his company,' said Roger Hurst.

'Well, I'm very sorry, sir, but Mr Arkwright is not available in until 2 pm. I can put you through to Mr Dawlish, our general manager.'

'No, I don't wish to speak to anyone else but Mr Arkwright regarding investments. I've been recommended by one of your investors to deal with Mr Arkwright personally.'

'I could make an appointment for you to see him from 2.30 pm.'

'Yes, that would be fine. Thank you.'

Hurst put the phone down. Then he took a large suitcase

out of the wardrobe, unlocked it and withdrew a grey wig, a thick grey beard and moustache, a pair of horn-rimmed glasses and a small flat cushion. He took from his wardrobe a long military-style raincoat, a blue serge suit, which was two sizes larger than his normal clothing, a white shirt, a plain blue tie, a blue woollen scarf, a grey snapped brim trilby and a pair of black Oxford shoes. He undressed down to his underclothing and put on the wig and moustache. He then tied the thin cushion in front of his stomach and put on the shirt and suit. He put on the tie with a Windsor knot. Next he put on his shoes, the raincoat, scarf and the trilby. Then, standing front of his wardrobe mirror, he studied the effect. He decided that he looked stouter and about 25 years older.

Hurst made himself a light lunch and watched the television until it was time to leave for his appointment. At 1.15 he looked out of his front window to see if any of his neighbours were about to see him leaving his flat in his disguise. There were none. Most were at work or having their midday meal indoors.

From the hallstand he took the heavy walking stick which served him as a weapon if he was assaulted by any of the people from whom he was collecting overdue loans. He quickly went to his car, which was conveniently parked in front of the block, and drove off.

He arrived at Arkwright's offices at 2.20 and knocked on Sharon's office door.

'Come in please, Mr Kilroy' said Sharon, rising from her desk to greet him.

Hurst entered the office and stood in the centre of the room, leaning on his walking stick.

'Please take a seat sir, and I'll see if Mr Arkwright is ready to receive you.'

Hurst sat down as if it were an effort, causing Sharon to give him a sympathetic look. Sharon spoke to Arkwright on the intercom and he responded, 'Please bring Mr Kilroy up, Sharon.'

'It's only one floor up, Mr Kilroy,' said Sharon, noting Hurst's awkwardness in mounting the stairs. When they arrived at Arkwright's office he was standing in the doorway.

'Please come in, Mr Kilroy,' said Arkwright, and to Sharon, 'I'll call you when Mr Kilroy is leaving.'

'Take a chair,' Arkwright said, indicating an easy chair in front of his huge but almost bare desk. Hurst took his hat off, hooked his walking stick on the back of the chair, settled himself down and looked around the sparsely-furnished office. A filing cabinet, a bookcase, two easy chairs and, surprisingly, a golf bag, stood in the corner of the room.

'Well, what can I do for you, Mr Kilroy?'

Hurst cleared his throat noisily before answering. 'I'd like to seek your advice regarding the making of a large investment. I have to admit that I have not been an investor in the past. I have a large amount of money in the bank, which I have bequeathed to my grandchildren. What I am hoping for is an opportunity to increase my capital so as to provide them with sufficient money to be able to raise mortgages to buy their own homes.'

Arkwright smiled broadly. 'What a commendable project, Mr Kilroy.'

'Well, I'm not in the best of health and it seemed the right thing for me to do before I shuffle off this mortal coil.'

'Oh, I'm sorry to hear that, but, yes, I do think you're doing the right thing. There are many developing companies attracting investments that promise to produce high dividends for their investors. What sort of amount do you wish to invest?'

Hurst cleared his throat and blew his nose with a large white handkerchief before he answered. 'Well, most of my wealth, I suppose. I shall keep a couple of hundred thousand in reserve to cover hospital and funeral expenses as they arise. The amount I'm willing to invest is likely to be something in excess of half a million pounds, Mr Arkwright.'

'Ah, that is a princely sum. I have just the company on our books to provide you with a safe and high yielding investment. It's the Offshore Wind Turbine Manufacturing Company. It has a history of success and promises to break all records in increasing its output of wind turbines.'

'That's really splendid, Mr Arkwright. It certainly sounds like the right sort of green company that deserves investment support.'

Arkwright forced a smile and mentally rubbed his hands. 'Would you like me to proceed with the necessary paperwork? When that's been done, all that is needed is the transfer of the amount to be paid into my business account for forwarding to the company and to issue the share certificates to you. Is there anything else you wish to discuss?'

'Actually, there is. I see you have a bag of golf clubs in the corner. They remind me of my golfing days. I played very often in my youth to middle years. Do you get much opportunity to play, Mr Arkwright?'

'Yes, I do, every morning from 8.30 to midday. By the way, since you are an old golfer, you may call me Albert.'

'Then call me Jack,' Hurst responded with a chuckle. 'I'd liked to see you playing. Where is your club? Perhaps I could follow you around in a buggy and then join you for lunch in the club house?'

'Yes, I'd be glad of your company. But I have to admit I don't like competition, so I always play alone, just to keep myself fit. Give me a ring when you want to watch me play and I'll reserve a buggy for you. Here, take this card, it has all the details about the club.' Arkwright handed the card across his desk.

'Well, thank you very much for putting me on the right course for making a profitable investment and I look forward to see you hole in one, Albert. Now I won't take up any more of your valuable time.' Hurst struggled to get up from the chair. Arkwright got up and handed Hurst his walking stick, which had fallen onto the floor. Then he buzzed for Sharon to come to the office.

Sharon arrived and as she led Hurst down the stairs, Arkwright called out, 'I'll in touch, Jack, cheerio for now.'

After Hurst had gone, Arkwright sat at his desk pondering over his latest client. This Kilroy chap seemed a bit of an oddball to have the amount of cash he was prepared to invest. But then not all wealthy people favour fashionable attire. And if he did go through with the investment, it would mean a sizeable commission for the firm. He just hoped that Kilroy wouldn't make a habit of visiting the golf club dressed as he had for their consultation.

\*\*\*

The following day Hurst drove to Hadley Golf Course and parked on the road in sight of the 14th hole, through the trees and shrubs that encircled the course. Crouching behind a thick bush, he scanned the fairway looking for golfers. Although it was a dry and unseasonably warm day, there were very few in sight.

Hurst checked the time; 10.45. He estimated that if Arkwright had teed off at 8.30 he should now be nearing the 13th tee. Fifteen minutes passed and Arkwright came in sight wheeling a golf trolley. He stopped at the tee area, pushed a tee into the ground, placed a golf ball on it and readied himself to strike the ball.

Hurst had seen enough. He returned to his car and drove home.

The following day he got up at 7 am. After completing his ablutions, he donned his disguise and had a light breakfast while watching the television news.

'Now to get the tools to finish the job,' he thought. He went into his bedroom, opened the wardrobe door and lifted a floorboard. He reached into the space and withdrew a small canvas holdall containing an automatic pistol wrapped in oily rags, a silencer and two magazines, each containing eight 9mm cartridges. The pistol was a Smith and Wesson Mk 22 Model Hush Puppy. It was a weapon used by US Navy Seals to kill sentries patrolling coastal areas when they came ashore on enemy beaches to mount covert attacks on coastal targets. Hurst had won the weapon and its accessories playing draw poker with a group of ex-Seals who had then been employed as security guards in the

Green Zone of Baghdad. He had smuggled the weapon into the UK when he had been sent home for a short spell of leave during the war with Iraq.

Hurst put on a pair of rubber gloves and polished every part of the gun. He did the same with the silencer and the two magazines. He did not need to clean the bullets, because he had not touched them since they had been loaded into the magazines by a Yankee jerk who had been bluffed into throwing in his hand, which had held a pair of jacks, by Hurst's pair of aces.

He inserted a magazine into the butt of the pistol and fitted the silencer to the barrel. Then he put the gun into the right-hand pocket of his raincoat and his binoculars into the left-hand pocket.

He checked his watch: 9.30. Time to go. He first looked out of his sitting room window to see if any of his neighbours were about who might see him leaving his flat. There was nobody in sight. He quickly went to his car, which was parked immediately outside the block, and drove away at high speed.

When he was nearing the golf club he turned off onto a little-used side road and pulled up on to a grass verge. He got out of the car and opened the boot. He lifted a mat from the floor of the boot and took out two clip-on false number plates. He closed the boot and quickly clipped them to the front and rear number plates, and got back into the car. He drove to the point where he had stopped on the previous day, got out of his car and walked through the trees and bushes to where he had crouched near the tee-off point for the 14th hole. He scanned the area with his binoculars, but only saw two golfers two hundred metres away. He hid behind a tree

and watched them playing for the 13<sup>th</sup> hole and teeing off
from the area he was watching. They were soon out of sight.
He checked his watch; it was now 10.38.

Just then Arkwright came in sight pulling a golf cart.
Hurst waited until Arkwright had reached the tee-off point,
pushed a tee into the ground, placed a golf ball on it and
readied himself to strike the ball. Then he emerged from
behind the tree.

'Good morning Mr Arkwright.'

Arkwright dropped his golf club and spun around to see
Hurst in his Jack Kilroy disguise.

'What are you doing here, Jack? You should have let me
know that you were coming this morning.'

Hurst gave a short laugh. 'If I'd have done that you
would have would had to introduce me to some of your fellow
golfers, and that would have spoiled my plans.'

'What on earth are you talking about? What plans?'
Arkwright said, beginning to realize that something was
very wrong. 'What in hell's name is this all about?'

'I've come to kill you, Albert. I killed your colleagues and
stole your money, and now I'm going to kill you.'

'Why do you want to kill me? I've done nothing to you!'
Arkwright said in a frenzied voice.

'Yes, I suppose I do owe you some sort of explanation,'
said Hurst. He drew his pistol from his pocket, stepped
forward and pointed it at Arkwright's forehead. 'Let me just
say, killing you is simply a means to an end.'

Hurst squeezed the trigger. The bullet tore through
Arkwright's head and took out the back of his skull, from
which spewed a stream of blood and brain tissue. Arkwright

fell backwards onto the golf trolley and the golf clubs and balls spilled out around his body.

'That was one helluva hole-in-one,' Hurst muttered, as he walked back to his car, whistling: *'This is a wonderful way to spend a morning, can't think of anything I'd rather do...'*

Before driving away, Hurst removed his hat, hairpiece, beard and moustache. When he reached the side road where he had clipped on the false number plates, he stopped, removed the false plates and hid them under the mat in the boot. He then drove home. On arrival he removed his outer clothing and changed into fashionable jeans, a check shirt and a leather jacket.

\*\*\*

About half an hour after Hurst had left the scene, two golfers approached the tee-off point where Arkwright's body lay..

'Good God, Tom, there's a body in the tee-off area,' said Reg.

They both bent down to examine the body.

'It looks like Albert Arkwright. Look at his head,' Tom said.

'Someone must have hit him with a golf ball,' Reg suggested.

Tom looked more closely. 'No, it must have been something harder than a golf ball to have made such a mess of his head. Look, there's a bullet hole in his forehead. Looks like his brains have been blown out of the back of his head.'

'Ugh, the sight of it is turning my guts over,' said Reg.

'Yes, ghastly. Must admit I got hardened to this sort of thing when I was in Iraq. Albert's been shot. I'll ring the police.' Tom took his mobile out of his jacket pocket. 'Keep your eyes open, Reg, the killer might still be on the course.'

Tom tapped in 999 and a voice answered, 'What is your emergency?'

'We're on the Hadley golf course and we've just found one of our members dead. It looks like he's been shot in the head.'

A few seconds passed and an authoritative voice came on the line. 'What is your name, and where exactly are you on the golf course?'

'I'm Tom Hewett and my golfing partner is Reg Collins. We're at the 14th tee.'

'Do you know who the victim is?'

'Yes, officer, it's Albert Arkwright.'

'Right, a team of police officers will be with you shortly. In the meantime stay where you are, don't touch the body and avoid moving around the immediate area.'

Tom and Reg moved away from the body and sat down on the grass.

The police officers duly arrived in several borrowed golf buggies. DCI Owen Warner, the officer in charge of the group, introduced himself to Hewett and Collins. He then had an area of about a hundred square metres taped off around the body. Accompanied by a medical officer, he examined the body. The doctor confirmed that the man had been shot dead within the last hour. Warner sent in a SOCO team to examine the body and the crime scene for forensic clues.

Derek Barnes, one of the SOCO team, shouted excitedly, 'Sir, I've found the bullet!'

'Fetch it here,' Warner ordered.

Barnes took it to Warner, who was talking to the doctor outside the taped-off area. Warner and the doctor were still wearing surgical gloves. Warner examined the misshapen bullet.

'I'd say this is probably a 9mm dumdum bullet,' Warner said, passing it to the doctor.

'Yes, I believe you're right. That would account for the extensive exit wound in the back of the victim's head.'

Warner returned the bullet to Barnes. 'Get this bagged and included with the rest of what's been found.'

'Judging by the amount of gunshot residue around the entry wound in his forehead, I'd say he was shot at very close range with a 9mm handgun,' said the doctor, who had served as a medical officer with the army for several years. 'As the exit wound appears to have been caused by a dumdum type of bullet, I would say the gun was a military weapon of the kind used by members of special force units to ensure their human targets are killed by one shot to the head. No doubt military armourers can advise if this is the case.'

When the SOCO team had completed all their tasks, Warner told the two coroner's officers to bag the body and place it in the ambulance that had been driven onto the course.

Before leaving the crime scene Warner told a uniformed sergeant who was present with the group to arrange for the scene to be protected by two constables until all local enquiries had been made.

On return to the borough police headquarters, DCI Warner reported to Alec Patton, Borough Commander, and Detective Superintendent Ralph Braddock. He gave them a full verbal report about the murder.

'Owen, I'd like you to take over the investigation into this murder, which to my mind is almost certainly linked to the murders of Rackman, Stratton and Hardwick,' said Commander Patton. 'Have DI Ahmed and DS Logan lead local enquiries at the golf club and local residents living near the club. In the meantime, Ralph, please arrange for a press conference to be arranged to ensure full media coverage. It might produce a response from members of the public who may have been in the area at the time of the shooting.'

The following morning DI Ahmed and his section drove out to the Golf Club to question club members. As there had been so few golfers on the course the previous day, nothing new was learned. The two golfers, Hewett and Collins, who had found the body, were again interviewed and their statements taken.

DC Sean Copling, a member of DI Ahmed's section, noticed a young boy kicking a football along the road outside the golf club.

'Hello, there sonny, would you like to help the police?' he said, showing the boy his warrant card.

The boy read the card and said, 'Are you a real detective?'

'Yes, I certainly am and my name is Sean. What's your name?'

'William Baker, but most people call me Billy. How can I help the police?'

'How old are you, Billy?'

'I'll be eleven next month.'

'Why aren't you at school?'

'Cos the heating's broke down and we were all sent home until it's fixed.'

'Were you playing around here yesterday?'

'Yes, this is where I like to kick my ball around.'

'Tell me, Billy, did you see anyone around here during the morning?'

Billy screwed up his face in thought. 'I only saw one old bloke getting out of his car.'

This could be what I want to hear, thought Copling. 'Now this is very important, Billy. Can you tell me what he looked like?'

'Oh, he was just an old geezer wearing a hat and a long raincoat.'

'What made him look old?'

'Uh, er, he had a grey beard and a walking stick.'

'What sort of car did he have?'

'It was an old grey one.'

'Did you see its number?'

'I saw three letters at the front of some numbers, which made a word. That's how I remember them,'

'What was the word, Billy?'

Billy's face reddened slightly. 'It was bum!'

'That's very useful information, Billy. Did you see where the old man went when he got out of his car?'

'He just walked onto the golf course.'

'Did you see or hear anything after he went on the golf course?'

Billy shook his head. 'No, I didn't see anything else. I buzzed off home to watch telly.'

'Well, Billy Baker, you've been very helpful to me and you deserve a reward, so here's a pound to buy some sweets.'

'Thanks, Sean,' Billy said and ran off to the nearest sweet shop.

DC Copling made a note of all Billy had said and reported to DS Logan.

'So it seems likely that the killer was an old man driving an old grey car, or a younger man disguised,' Logan said. 'If it was a younger man, my guess is that it was that ex-soldier Robert Carson. Carry on with the house-to-house enquiries, Sean. I'll let the inspector know what you got from that kid.'

***

As a result of the press conference an elderly man named Edgar Hughes came forward and told the desk sergeant that he had been walking his dog near the golf course at the time the murder was committed. The sergeant rang DCI Warner, who came down, accompanied by DI Ahmed, to interview Hughes. He led him into an interview room and invited him to sit down opposite him and Ahmed at the table. He then introduced himself and Ahmed to Hughes.

'Now, Mr Hughes, I understand that you may have some information about a man you saw on or near the Hadley Golf Course yesterday.'

'Yes, Detective Chief Inspector Warner, and I hope you'll find it's useful. Being the coordinator of our neighbourhood watch scheme, I'm always alert to any strange occurrences. After hearing Detective Superintendent Braddock's appeal on television, I thought it only right that I should report to the police about what I had seen and heard near the scene of the crime and...'

'And what was it that you did see and hear, Mr Hughes?' Warner asked.

'As I was about to explain to you, I was walking my Cocker Spaniel, his name is Rover, near the trees and bushes around the golf course. I heard a man whistling and stopped to see him passing quite close to me, but not apparently seeing me.'

'Can you describe the man you saw?'

'Oh, yes, he looked quite old. He was above average height and rather overweight. He wore spectacles and his hair and beard were grey. He was dressed in an old-fashioned way, trilby hat and long raincoat, but in spite of his physical appearance and attire I didn't get the impression that he was as old as he looked.'

'Why did you think that, Mr Hughes?' Warner asked, beginning to feel like yawning.

'Well, he was carrying a walking stick, but he wasn't using it.'

'What was he doing with it then?' Warner interjected.

Hughes put on a hurt look. 'He was just waving it about as he marched out of the golf course like a guardsman, whistling *This is a wonderful way to spend an evening*' or something like that.'

'Did you see him getting into a car?'

'No, I was walking away from him, but I did hear a car roaring away a couple of minutes later.'

Ahmed had been making notes during the interview and produced a written statement form, which he read over to Hughes. 'Can you confirm that this is what you said, Mr Hughes?'

Hughes read the statement as Moses might have first read the Ten Commandments. 'Yes, Detective Inspector Ahmed, that is exactly what I said. I must congratulate you on your very neat handwriting.'

'Then will you please sign the statement immediately under the last line of text,' Ahmed said, passing him a black ballpoint pen. Hughes signed the statement with a flourish and passed it back to Ahmed.

'Thank you, Mr Hughes, your information should be helpful in identifying the man you saw,' said Warner.

'Will that be all then, Detective Chief Inspector?'

'Yes, for the present, but we may need to ask you to attend an identification parade at some future date.'

'I'm really pleased that I have been able to help you solve your case. It'll be something I can report to my neighbourhood watch group at our next monthly meeting.'

Warner forced a smile. Hughes got up to leave and Ahmed led Hughes out of the police station.

'Cheerio, Mr Hughes,' said Ahmed.

'Goodbye, Detective Inspector Ahmed,' Hughes said as he walked away to catch a bus.

Ahmed joined Warner in his office with a broad grin. 'Where does that leave us, guv?'

'To be frank, I just don't know. But I hope we don't unearth any more witnesses like Hughes.

Mr Hughes. Regretfully, I'm beginning to wonder if DS Logan is right in his belief that Carson is the killer.'

'Yes, but we've absolutely no real evidence that Carson is our man.'

'But we do need to know where he was yesterday morning, Samier, so you and Logan had better call on him.

If he's guilty we might be able to screw a confession out of him if we put the pressure on.'

'Right, I'll pick up Logan and visit Carson.'

Ahmed and Logan drove to Carson's flat in Romford. Logan rang the bell and seconds later Carson opened the door. Ahmed and Logan produced their warrant cards for Carson's inspection.

'I don't know why you bother with that performance every time you come here,' said Carson. 'And with all your comings and goings, my neighbours will begin to think I'm taking in lodgers. Come in.' He led them into the sitting room. 'Take a seat, detectives, and tell me what it is you want to know now.'

'We'll not take up much of your time, Mr Carson. We would just like to know exactly where you were between 8 am and midday yesterday.'

'I was here, alone, as I always am these days.'

'Is there anyone who can verify that you were here Mr Carson?' Logan said, his hand poised to make notes in his pocketbook.

'No there isn't, Sergeant. As I've told you people several times before, I live alone and rarely go out in the morning. So, if that's all you wanted to know, please leave now, because there's something I particularly want to see on television and the programme starts in ten minutes.'

Ahmed rose from the sofa and Logan followed suit.

'I do apologize for disturbing your evening's entertainment, Mr Carson, but you must realize we're investigating a series of brutal murders and because of your unfortunate experience with the victims, you have to be regarded as a possible suspect,' Ahmed said.

Carson stood up, braced his shoulders and looked straight at Ahmed. 'If you're looking for suspects for the killing of those crooked stockbrokers, there're scores of them. And just because most of them are wealthy, have been to public schools and universities and live in grand houses doesn't mean that they are incapable of murder.'

Logan moved in front of Ahmed and said in a loud voice, 'Just hang on there, Carson. The man who was killed yesterday was shot in the head. We've established that the weapon was a military automatic pistol with a silencer attached, loaded with eight 9mm dumdum bullets. Now as you must be aware...'

'That's enough, Sergeant, back off and get outside!' Ahmed shouted.

Logan slunk out of the room and slammed the front door as he left.

'I really must apologize for my colleague's tactless behaviour,' said Ahmed. 'I'll let myself out. Goodnight, Mr Carson.'

'Goodnight to you, Inspector, and I hope I shan't see you and that sergeant of yours here again.'

# CHAPTER THIRTY-SEVEN

Carson was half watching a re-run of the film *Three Kings,* an over-hyped American movie set in the 2003 war with Iraq. The front door bell rang. He rose reluctantly and opened the front door to see Hurst standing on the doorstep. He was wearing his military raincoat and a baseball cap.

'To what do I owe this unannounced visit?' Carson asked.

'Oh, sorry, Bob, I forgot your rule about visiting - always ring before you visit.'

'Never mind the bullshit, come in and take off your coat and that ridiculous hat.'

'This headgear is very fashionable. Everybody wears them' Hurst replied, as he hung his hat and coat on the hallstand.

'Fashionable is simply a word to make clothing and accessories more marketable, Roger,' Carson said as he led Hurst into the sitting room.

Hurst didn't have an answer to Carson's homespun

philosophy. 'What's this you're watching, Bob?' he asked as he made himself comfortable on the sofa.

'Oh, just another fairy story about the Iraq War. Do you want to watch it?'

'No thanks, that's one war I want to forget.'

Carson switched off the television and went to drinks cabinet. 'Is it the usual poison for you, Roger?'

'Yes, in a large glass, please.'

Carson poured two doubles into appropriately-sized glasses and brought them to the sofa table.

'Cheers,' said Hurst, taking a deep swig from his glass.

'Cheerio, Roger,' answered Carson, taking a sip from his.

'So, what's new with you Bob?'

Carson shrugged. 'Nothing much worth mentioning, but I did get a visit from that Pakistani detective inspector and his overbearing sergeant. They seem to be convinced that I'm a murderer.'

'What did they want this time?'

'They wanted to know where I was yesterday morning.'

'Did you tell them?'

'Yes, I did, and in no uncertain manner. The inspector is a reasonable chap, but that sergeant was doing his best to connect me with the murder weapon, which he described as some sort of military automatic pistol with a silencer attached. The inspector gave him a reprimand and told him to get out. He then apologised to me for the sergeant's tactless manner. I told him I hoped I'd seen the last of them.'

'Huh, all coppers are the same. If they can't get the goods on you they'll try to cook up a case against you.'

'From my experience, I can't say that I see the police, civil or military, to all be like that, but if you don't mind I'd rather talk about something different.'

'Then what about this for starters, Bob. Your birthday's at the end of the month, so what about a trip out for a lash-up meal to celebrate the occasion?'

Carson shook his head. 'No thanks. I think I'd rather stay at home and have a long chat on the phone with my daughter Janice and my grandchildren in Australia. They keep asking when I'm going to get down under.'

'So, you'll not want my company on that day then, Bob?'

'No, I'll give you a ring when I want your company, Bob.'

'Okay, point taken. I'll await your summons. In the meantime, what about another drink? All this talking has made me thirsty.'

Carson took his glass, poured a triple measure of whisky into it and handed it to him.

'Aren't you having another?'

'No, I've had enough. When you go I want to make my telephone call to Oz.'

'Is that a broad hint for me to leave, Bob?'

'Yes, I suppose it is. When I've had my call I'm turning in. All the attention I'm getting from the police is rather wearying.'

'I fully understand your position. When I've finished this drink and made necessary use of your bog, I'll shuffle off into the night.'

While Hurst was finishing his drink, Carson switched the television on to see a news programme. After the daily ration of political news and the interview of a popular celebrity, a detective superintendent was shown being interviewed by a tabloid newspaper reporter. The reporter was pressing the superintendent for an answer regarding the slow progress in investigating the murder of three stockbrokers. The superintendent said that a former senior police detective, who had been working as a private detective, had been employed by one of the murder victims to investigate a particular suspect. The detective had also been murdered. The superintendent refused to name the suspect and said the police were making determined efforts solve the case, but that they had been hampered by having to question a very large number of people who had dealings with the murdered stockbrokers and had to be considered as possible suspects.

Carson switched off the television. 'Do you see what I mean, Roger? I'm that "particular suspect" in the case, simply because I'm an ex-soldier who has been trained to kill with whatever weapon that was available to me.'

'The police have got a very flimsy case, Bob. There are thousands of ex-soldiers who have been trained to kill. Me included,' Hurst replied with a humourless laugh.

'Yes, but presumably none of the people who invested with the murdered stockbrokers have either been in the army or fought and killed in a war zone.'

Hurst gave a slight shrug. 'I shouldn't bother yourself, Bob, the police haven't got any tangible evidence against you. They'll soon drop you and find another suspect to investigate. Now I must use your loo before I leave,' Hurst said, after draining his glass.

Hurst left the room and closed the sitting room door. He went to the bathroom and pulled a piece of toilet paper off the roll. He clasped it in his hand and took an ammunition magazine from his inside pocket. Keeping the toilet paper wrapped around it, he placed it behind several bottles and packets in the bathroom cabinet. He flushed the toilet and returned to the sitting room.

'I'm off now, Bob. Thanks for the drinks. I'll be seeing you when you're at home for callers. If I don't see you before your birthday, I hope you have a happy one.'

Carson followed Hurst into the passage and watched him putting his raincoat and hat on.

He opened the front door and Hurst went out.

'Goodnight, Bob.'

'Goodnight, Roger,' Carson replied.

Returning to the sitting room, Carson picked up the telephone and dialled Janice's number. She answered the phone almost immediately.

'Now that is an extraordinary coincidence, Dad. I was just about to ring you with some very good news.'

'How are you all, Janice?'

'We're in great shape, and you?'

'Making out, but still being badgered by the police. But never mind all that, what's the news?'

'You'd better sit down to hear it, Dad.'

'I'm sitting, Janice and all agog.'

'Ben has won the first prize in the Australian national lottery!'

'Wow! That is good news. Does he know how much he's won?'

'Yes, it's more than four million dollars!'

'I'm so happy for you, Janice. Ben will now be able to afford the specialist treatment and operation he needs.'

'Yes, that's right. Ben is going to arrange for the extension to be built. You won't have to wait for it to be finished before you come out here. We've a sofa bed in the sitting room, so you can sleep in there. As you're such an early riser, we won't be inconvenienced in any way. Get your flight booked as soon as you can. We're all looking forward to the day you arrive.'

'There's just one snag, Janice. I don't think the police will let me leave the country until they can rule me out of their investigations.'

'Well you haven't murdered anyone, Dad, so why should they make you their suspect?'

'It's a very long story, which I'll tell you all about when I arrive. May I have a word with Ben and the children now?'

'I'm afraid not, Dad, the children are at school and Ben is still sleeping. It's 8.40 am here. You've forgotten the time difference.'

'Never mind then, just remember me to Ben and give the children a big hug from me when they come home.'

'I will, Dad. Look after yourself and do what you can to get here as soon as you can.'

'Don't worry about that, I shall. Goodbye, Janice.'

Carson made a cup of coffee and sat meditating over Janice's news. What great news - and to think that they were going to share their good fortune with him. He just hoped he could get the police off his back and join his family. It was such a great pity that Valerie wasn't there to share the family's happiness. He would visit the police tomorrow and see if they would let him leave the country.

Suddenly Carson felt able to take on any challenge that he might have to face. It took him a long time to get to sleep that night.

# CHAPTER THIRTY-EIGHT

Carson rose early, for there was much to be done. He climbed out of the shower and dried himself. Then he put on his underclothes and went to the bathroom cabinet to get his razor, brush and shaving soap. He would need to get this lot sorted out.

He rummaged through Valerie's toiletries to find a packet of razor blades and found them wedged between a large bottle of shampoo and a box of toilet soap. As he pulled the packet of razor blades free, his hand caught the top of a bottle of shampoo. It fell out of the cupboard and dropped onto a thick bathroom mat. It didn't break, and Carson picked it up to replace it in the cupboard. Then he noticed that there was something in the cupboard that shouldn't be there; a parcel of what looked like toilet roll. Peeping out from it he could see the end of the magazine of an automatic pistol. He could just see a cartridge at the top of it. He thought for a moment, then replaced the bottle where it had been and had his shave.

When he was fully dressed and eating his breakfast, he pondered over his find. Since Hurst was the only person who had availed himself of the bathroom, he had to be the one who had hidden the magazine in the cupboard. But why? Fortunately, by a stroke of luck, he had found the magazine before the police. Was Hurst expecting the police to obtain a warrant to search his home for weapons? Perhaps he even intended to make an anonymous call to the police. The fact that Hurst had a loaded magazine surely meant that he had been the person who had killed Arkwright and the others. He must get in touch with Detective Inspector Ahmed, the one detective who had shown that he was doubtful about Carson's guilt.

After breakfast Carson rang the police station on his land-line telephone. The phone was answered by a control room operator. 'Who's calling please?' she asked.

'My name is Robert Carson and I should like to speak to Detective Inspector Ahmed.'

'Hold on, sir, I'll check if he's available.' A minute passed and the operator came back on the line. 'Yes, he's in the building and I'm transferring your call.'

Carson said 'thank you' and waited for Ahmed to speak.

'Good morning, Mr Carson. This is a bit of a surprise for you to be telephoning me after our last meeting. So what's it all about?'

'I should like you to come to my home, where I have something you should see. I might also be able to convince you that I can identify the murderer of Arkwright and the others.'

'This all seems to be rather irregular. If you wish to make a statement you should present yourself here.'

'Never mind the irregularity. On this occasion, I can assure you that what I want to show you is important evidence in support of your investigation.'

'Hmm, I'll have to check with my boss first. If he is agreeable I'll come to your home later this morning.'

'Good, I look forward to your arrival. I promise you won't be disappointed, Inspector.'

As soon as the line cleared, Carson rang Hurst. He was surprised that the phone was answered.

'Who is it?' Hurst asked.

'It's Bob. I didn't expect you to be at home, Roger. I was going to leave you a message.'

'I've taken a few days' leave. What's the message?'

'I've changed my mind about going out for a treat on my birthday. I've booked lunch for two at the Savoy Hotel on the 31$^{st}$, which is a Saturday. Are you interested?'

'Lunch at the Savoy, eh? You are going a bit upmarket aren't you, Bob?'

'Yes and why not? As it happens, I've had some good news from Australia. I hope to be going out there soon.'

'Well, if you'll be saying goodbye soon, how could I refuse your invitation? Remind me nearer the time and I'll get my best suit cleaned.'

'What are you plans for today, Roger, doing anything special?'

'No nothing very much, I'll be watching TV most of the day and then I'll probably go out to my local later.'

'OK, Roger, keep in touch.'

***

As soon as Ahmed had finished with Carson's call, he reported to Detective Superintendent Braddock. DCI Warner was with Braddock discussing everything they had on file about the four murders.

'Join us, Samier,' Braddock said. 'We're going over this bloody quadruple murder case.'

'Actually, that's exactly why have come to see you, sir.'

'Why, have you come up with something we don't know about?'

'Yes I have, sir.' Ahmed told Braddock and Warner everything he had been told by Carson. Braddock and Warner looked at each other, nodded slowly and then turned to Ahmed. 'Well, you certainly do know something we don't,' Braddock said.

'Can I do as Carson has asked, sir?'

'You certainly can, but DCI Warner will accompany you and take the lead. Is that all right with you, Owen?'

'It certainly is, boss. I'd do anything to get this case wrapped up. If we could get a warrant it would be a good opportunity to search Carson's place.'

'Then get one straight away. Everybody has Carson in the frame for the killings, so you'll have no trouble getting a warrant. You, Ahmed, get a small team together, comprising DS Lord and a couple of DCs, including Copling. He's firearms trained, isn't he?'

'Yes, sir, but is it necessary for armed officers to attend?' Ahmed said.

'It certainly is, because if Carson is the killer he is well armed and we need to be ready for anything. I'll sign a request for an automatic pistol to be issued to DC Copling.'

DCI Warner got his warrant and DC Copling was issued

with a Glock 17 automatic pistol by the firearms training inspector. It was early afternoon when Ahmed rang Carson to tell him that he was on his way and that DCI Warner and three other officers would be with him.

When they arrived, Warner produced a search warrant and handed it to Carson. 'We need to search this house,' he said.

'Oh, okay, search away. Are you looking for anything in particular?' If you are I can show you a good starting point.'

'And where's that?' Warner asked.

'In the bathroom,' Carson said, leading him and Ahmed into the bathroom.

Carson opened the cupboard and took out the bottle of shampoo and box of soap. There lay the magazine. Warner took a pair of rubber gloves from his pocket and put one on his right hand. He picked up the magazine and showed it to Ahmed. Then, turning to Carson, he said, 'Is this some sort of confession you're going to give us? If it is, where's the gun?' Handing the magazine to DC Holt, who was wearing rubber gloves in preparation for searching the house, he said, 'Take this to SOCO and get them to check for fingerprints immediately.'

Holt bagged the gun and left the house.

'My guess is that you'll not find any fingerprints on that magazine,' said Carson. 'I've never touched it and the man who put it there will have made sure his fingerprints were not on it when he put it in that cupboard.'

'So, you're telling me it's not yours, but that you know who put it there?' Warner said

'Yes, it was put there last night by Roger Hurst,' Carson replied.

'How can you be so sure Hurst put it there?' Ahmed interjected.

'Simply because he is the only man, other than me, to have used my bathroom since I moved into this house.'

Warner looked puzzled. 'What possible motive could this man Hurst have to do such a thing?'

DS Lord entered the room with DC Copling. 'Apart from the bathroom we've searched everywhere and haven't found anything of a suspicious nature, sir,' Lord said.

'Thank you, Debra,' Warner replied.

'You ask me what motive Hurst had to plant the magazine in my bathroom. If you'd all like to sit down I'll make you coffee and answer all of your questions,' said Carson.

Warner and Ahmed exchanged knowing looks, and Ahmed nodded.

'Very well, Mr Carson, never mind the coffee, but we'll listen to your explanation and hope that it won't be a lot of bunkum in an effort to get you off the hook.'

'You'll get no bunkum from me, Chief Inspector.'

'Then fire away, Mr Carson,' Warner said, as he sat down on Carson's favourite armchair. The other three detectives sat on the settee. DS Lord took her pocket book and a pen from her shoulder bag.

'Who is this man Hurst? He obviously isn't a friend.'

'You're right, he's no friend of mine. To explain I have to go back to 2003, to when Hurst and I were serving in Iraq. We were in the same battalion. He was a platoon sergeant and I was the battalion RSM. Following a bloody action with an Iraqi unit, of company strength, when Hurst's platoon commander was badly wounded and two of his men were killed. Hurst's men captured an Iraqi NCO. As there was no field intelligence officer or senior NCO available to question the prisoner, Hurst took it upon himself to question the man, who would only give his number, rank and name. Hurst became enraged by the prisoner's defiance and beat him unmercifully until he nearly died of his injuries. One of Hurst's men, who witnessed the beating of the prisoner, reported the incident to me and I intervened and had Hurst arrested. Later, when Hurst was being questioned by his company commander, a major, and an SIB NCO, Hurst became very aggressive and struck the major in the face, breaking his nose. A field general court martial was held, at which I attended as the primary prosecution witness. The soldier who reported Hurst's action to me had been killed by friendly fire before the court martial. Hurst was stripped of his rank, sentenced to 112 days' field punishment and discharged with ignominy. As a result he lost his service pension and his wife deserted him. I subsequently learned that Hurst had told his fellow prisoners that he'd 'get even with that fucking sergeant major one of these days.'

'Are you getting all this down, Debra?' Warner interposed.

'Yes, sir, in shorthand. I'll type it up later.'

'Carry on, Mr Carson,' Warner said.

'When I retired last January, I met Hurst in the British Legion Club at Romford. He immediately tried to ingratiate himself with me. I was going through a bad time, having just lost my wife at a very early age. Like Hurst, who had no family or friends, I was very lonely. He seemed to have put the past behind him and because of his apparent change of character I felt sorry for him and a rather half-hearted relationship developed between us.'

'Warner leaned forward and looked directly at Carson. 'If Hurst secretly hid his hatred for you, why didn't he kill you?'

'If he had done so, my previous connection with him would have come to light and he would have become the prime suspect. By killing Rackman and the others he was establishing what he thought was a perfect frame-up against me.'

'If what you have told us is true, then Hurst must surely be nothing less than a homicidal maniac,' Ahmed said.

'Well, I have to say I'm convinced, but we need to get verification about the incidents in Iraq, which no doubt can be obtained from MOD (Army) and Mr Carson's former battalion commander. I'll leave you to deal with that, Samier.'

The front door bell rang. 'See who that is, Holt,' Warner said.

Holt went to the door and a minute later returned with DC Copling.

'What's the score on the fingerprints, Sean?' Warner asked.

'SOCO thoroughly checked the magazine and said there was no trace of any fingerprints on it, sir.'

'Well, our next step is to pay a visit to Mr Hurst, if he's at home,' Warner said.

'I rang him before you came, Chief Inspector. He told me he was on holiday and was staying at home all day.'

'You didn't mention that you had found his magazine, did you?' Warner asked.

'Of course not. If I'd done so, he'd have known the game was up.'

'Since it's likely that he is still armed with an automatic pistol, we'd better arrange for a firearms team to provide back-up. Mr Carson, let me have Hurst's address.'

Carson wrote the address on a piece of paper and handed it to Warner.

'Debra, go back to the station and transcribe those shorthand notes into a statement for Mr Carson to sign later. Ahmed, you and I will go to this address and park out of sight of the block of flats where Hurst lives. He's in a ground floor flat, which will make it easier for us to approach. I'll get on to the superintendent and put him in the picture and ask him to authorise the engagement of the firearms team. Copling, Holt, you two won't be needed, so report back to your section sergeant.'

'What about me, Chief Inspector, am I free to go?' Carson asked.

'Not yet, Mr Carson. Please call in to the station later today to sign your statement and answer a few more questions. We might then be able to rule you out as a suspect in this case.'

Detective Superintendent Braddock authorised the use of the firearms team and told Warner that he would attend the scene with him. If Hurst was the killer of his former mentor and friend, he wanted to be in on the action.

An hour later the three senior detectives approached Hurst's flat. The six-man firearms team drove opposite the block of flats in an unmarked van to wait for Braddock's signal to deploy for possible action.

Ahmed rapped on the flat front door. A few seconds passed and the door was partially opened to reveal Hurst, unshaven and bleary-eyed and wearing a dressing gown.

Ahmed produced his warrant card and showed it to Hurst. But before Ahmed could utter a word, Hurst shouted, 'What do you want, coppers?' He had seen Braddock and Warner behind Ahmed.

'We are here to talk to you about your possible illegal possession of a firearm.'

'That's a load of bullshit, copper. I don't have any illegal firearms, so you can piss off.'

Braddock walked up to the door and drove his foot against it, knocking Hurst off-balance. He then signalled the firearms team to get out of the van and take up positions behind the low walls which faced the block of flats.

'You now have six marksmen aiming their weapons at you, so throw your gun out and come out of the flat with your hands over your head,' Braddock shouted.

'You can go fuck yourself, because you're not going to take me alive to spend any more time in prison,' Hurst screamed back, as he slammed the door shut.

Braddock and Warner kicked at the door until it opened. Braddock then signalled the firearms team to advance and enter the flat. The sergeant in charge of the firearms team led his men in to search each room.

As they were about to enter Hurst's bedroom, they heard a single shot. The sergeant entered and saw Hurst lying on his back, with a massive hole in the top of his head. The ceiling and the bedroom wall behind him were covered with blood and brain tissue.

The sergeant went out of the room and shouted, 'He's dead!' Braddock, Warner and Ahmed joined him and they went into the bedroom.

'He's performed the classic method of suicide, gun in mouth to blow the top of your head off. There's not much chance of failure that way,' Braddock said sarcastically.

\*\*\*

Ahmed obtained the information regarding Hurst's court martial in Iraq from the MOD and Carson and Hurst's former commanding officer in Iraq. The gun used by Hurst was identified as the weapon that had killed Arkwright. The finding of over £100,000 pounds in Hurst's hidey-hole in his wardrobe was identified by its wrapping as the money that had been stolen from the Arkwright brokerage's safe.

As a result of the further questioning of Carson and the partial identification of Hurst and his clothing by Mr Edgar Hughes, Carson was completely exonerated from any involvement with the murders. Carson was visited by the Borough Commander and other police officers who had been involved in the investigation. They wished him well and hoped that he'd have success in his bid to emigrate to Australia.

# CHAPTER THIRTY-NINE

The day after Carson had been cleared to leave the country, he couldn't wait to telephone Janice to tell her he was free to proceed with his emigration to Australia.

'That's wonderful news, Dad. Get your visa and book your flight as soon as you can.'

'I'll do that straight away. I've only got to hand over this house to the owner. I'll not be burdened much with luggage. I'll buy what I need in the way of clothing when I arrive.'

'Yes, Dad we'll make you a real bonzer Aussie when you get here,' Janice said with a little laugh.

'Goodbye for now darling, and love to all. I'll be with you soon.'

'Goodbye, Dad, love from all.'

\*\*\*

The next day Carson arranged with the owner for the handover of the house. He agreed to carry out the takeover the day before he was to leave the country. Carson obtained an Australian visa to enter the country. Next he went to the nearest travel agency to book a first-class flight to Sydney, Australia.

'How soon would you like to go?' The agency clerk enquired.

'As soon as possible, please.'

'I can fit you in on a flight to Sydney in two days' time,' she replied.

'Yes, that'll be fine.'

'I'll need to clear it with the airline, sir. Can you come in tomorrow morning, around ten o'clock, to settle the account and collect your ticket and other paperwork?'

'Certainly, I'll be here promptly at 10.00 hours,' Carson replied with a laugh.

When he got home he rang the owner of the estate agency that managed the property on behalf of the owner and asked if they could carry out their necessary checks the following day, at 9 am. They agreed.

Carson spent the afternoon packing essential clothing and personal items he couldn't bear to part with. He put all the clothing, bed linen and oddments he wasn't taking to Australia in large plastic sacks and took them to a local Oxfam shop.

Next morning he got up very early to ensure that everything was clean and in order for the handover. The agent arrived on time and was well satisfied with the state of the house. He agreed that Carson could hand the keys of the house to the estate agency that evening. Carson intended booking one night at a hotel near Gatwick airport.

Carson arrived at the travel agency at 9.55 am. He

settled the account and collected the flight ticket and other papers and left the agency still clutching them in his left hand. He was in a state of euphoria. At last, after all the tragedy and turmoil he had experienced since leaving the army, his life was now showing a promise of happiness. He couldn't contain his excitement at the thought of going to Australia to join his beloved family.

Seeing a café across the road, he remembered that he hadn't eaten that morning. He decided to drop in for a coffee and a quick snack; it would give him a chance to read through the papers he'd been given at the agency.

Just as he stepped out on to the zebra crossing, his mobile phone rang. He took the call, only to find that it was simply his phone provider ringing with an offer of a special contract. He returned the phone to his pocket and continued to cross, but the call had taken his attention away from the road for a moment, and before he had time to react he realised that a speeding car was bearing down on him at high speed.

There was no time to avoid the impact. Bob was hurled several yards to land on the pavement kerb. He lay inert in a gathering pool of blood, his travel documents dropping from his lifeless fingers and swirling away in the breeze.

Bob Carson would not be needing them now.